A REBEL'S BEACON

A Sweet Adventure Romance

SARA BLACKARD

Chapter One

THE TURQUOISE WATERS of Resurrection Bay stretched out before Bjørn Rebel as he flew toward the mountains. The stick of his new AW139 helicopter he'd affectionately named Annie hummed beneath his hands as he scanned the console and eased his pretty girl along the coast to where the sea lions lounged. An eagle swooped down to its nest and stood regally on the edge, watching their approach. Bjørn adjusted his speed and turned to the couple behind him.

"If you look out the right, we're about to pass our nation's mascot." Bjørn couldn't contain his joy as it stretched across his face. "This bald eagle is guarding its nest. We could even catch a glimpse of any hatchlings that might be in there."

Could he really be in Seward, Alaska, taking his first customers on a wildlife tour? In what little downtime the army gave him as a member of the 160th Special Operations Aviation Regiment—otherwise known as Night Stalkers—he'd planned, made lists, sketched logos, and rewrote taglines. He'd filled notebooks full of ideas and budgets for so many years, he had wondered if it would ever actually happen.

He pulled back on the cyclic some more. The chopper responded like it was an extension of himself. Excitement burst like sunshine in his chest, and he chuckled low.

He'd have to thank his brother-in-law, Marshall Rand, for providing such a sweet replacement for the helicopter the terrorists blew up while trying to capture Marshall and his son, Carter. A piece of Bjørn's heart had exploded when he watched his first bird burst into a fiery ball of flames. Sure, insurance had covered the damage, but Bjørn had searched for over a year for the perfect chopper within his price range. Now, because of Marshall's generosity, the money from the insurance claim, and what he'd saved while in the military, Bjørn had the best helicopter on the market and enough money to float him for several years while he built up his business.

He hovered at the perfect location for the couple to view the eagle and the nest and keep enough distance not to disturb the animal. The majestic bird just ruffled its feathers and shifted its stance, turning its head away like a huge, metal beast wasn't something it needed to worry about. Another eagle flapped up from the ocean with a silver fish in its talons, and the woman in the backseat gasped.

"Henry, look!" Her enthusiastic tone turned Bjørn's head to watch their amazement.

He loved that about witnessing people experiencing things for the first time. Their excitement made all the planning and stress worth it and helped him see situations from a new angle. Would he ever tire of it, eventually seeing the beauty Alaska offered as just another day at work? He hoped not.

"Oh, eagle babies!" The woman shrieked, shaking Henry's arm, and Bjørn checked out the windshield to hide his laughter.

"Yeah. Cool." Henry's lack of enthusiasm needled under Bjørn's skin. "Christy, I thought you said this was an adventure tour."

Bjørn clenched his teeth as he pushed on the sticks to get them moving again, glancing in the mirror that showed the passenger area. Nothing irked him more than ungrateful people. They hadn't even flown a mile from Seward, and the dude was already complaining.

This might be where Bjørn's downfall would come. For the last ten years, he'd flown soldiers into dangerous missions that would curl most people's toes. He'd transported more fallen heroes back to base than he cared to think about. Listening to pampered tourists complain when they didn't have a clue what real suffering was like might just test Bjørn's patience to the limit.

"Knock it off, Henry. Just because I didn't want to fish *again* doesn't mean you have to be a jerk." Christy's spunk had Bjørn wanting to pump his fist in the air. "Besides, you kept complaining about the choppy waters. I figured a change in pace would be nice."

"It's that stupid boat captain's fault for taking us to the roughest spot in the entire bay," Henry whined like a two-year-old.

So, the dude was one of those people who blamed everything on everyone else. Bjørn couldn't stand people like that. His parents had drilled into him and his six siblings that a person who took responsibility for their actions and shortcomings was a person others could trust.

"Why did I bring you on *my* dream trip again? I'm having a hard time remembering." Christy's comment made Bjørn's gut twist. She didn't deserve to be treated like this on her vacation.

"Because you wanted to stick it to good ol' Pops." Henry's sneer tempted Bjørn to turn in the seat and slam his fist in the jerk's face.

"So, you two have weak stomachs?" Bjørn glanced over his shoulder, not really worried since Annie flew smooth like butter, but more to stop the unhappy couple before a fight broke out.

"Man, there's nothing weak in me." Henry puffed up his chest like a challenged ape.

Christy rolled her eyes, looked at Bjørn, pointed her finger at her boyfriend, and mouthed, "Big baby." Bjørn smirked, turning in his seat before the baby could see. The ocean churned before them, giving him an idea.

"Since you two have stomachs of steel, I'd like to show you something." Bjørn hoped Henry could hear the challenge in his voice.

"Bring it on, man." Male ego almost filled the cockpit.

Henry didn't know what strength was, and Bjørn wouldn't mind giving the jerk a lesson on humility. Tilting Annie onto her side, Bjørn circled the bubbling water at the required distance from the whale pod below. Sure, he could've just hovered, but where was the adventure in that? A team of humpback whales breached through the bubble-net they'd created, snatching up herring and other little fish. Christy clapped as the huge mammals bobbed up and down in the water.

Bjørn sped up through the last rotation and straightened Annie in the opposite direction from their destination. "We still good?"

"Yeah." Henry's tan had paled on his face.

"That was amazing." Christy glanced through the window behind them like she could still see the whales.

"Now, I normally don't offer this since most people can't handle it, but you two seem the adventurous types." Bjørn almost snorted as Henry's Adam's apple bobbed in the mirror. "I have some tricks I learned in the army flying special ops I can show you, if you like."

"Really?" Christy bounced in her seat. "You'd actually do it with us in here?"

"If you're up for it." Bjørn shrugged. "Of course, if you tell anyone, I'll deny it."

"We are absolutely up for it." Christy didn't even look at Henry.

"Whatever," Henry muttered, tightening his hold on the harness straps.

Bjørn pushed down the gleeful expression and jammed the stick to the side, flipping the helicopter in a roll. Christy screamed, a smile stretching across her face. Henry's eyes widened as the color leeched from his face.

"We good?" Bjørn leveled back out and looked in the mirror for the answer.

"Yes!" Christy's yell made him chuckle, while Henry nodded reluctantly beside her.

"You sure?" Bjørn raised his eyebrow in challenge.

"I can handle anything you dish out." Henry glared at Bjørn's reflection.

"Just in case, there are barf bags in the pocket on the

side of your seat." Bjørn shrugged, then glanced around, making a big deal about pretending to be lost. "Oh, wait. We're going the wrong way."

He maneuvered the cyclic and collective, causing the chopper to do a back flip, rotating halfway through the flip so the nose pointed the opposite direction. Christy's squeal filled with laughter, forcing one from Bjørn's chest. A glance in the mirror found Henry suppressing his gags.

Bjørn pushed the helicopter faster, the expansive blue-green of the ocean skimming past below them, increasing to top speed as they approached the glacier's face. He angled his girl up when it looked like they would hit the ice block and rocketed toward the clouds.

"Wahoo!" Christy screamed from the back, mirroring his own excitement.

He shot past the glacier's top, reaching higher into the sky. Finally, he flipped the bird backward and dived toward earth. He loved flying. Loved the rush of adrenaline only found behind the stick of his pretty girl.

"Oh, no," was the only warning before Henry's retching filled the cockpit.

"This is totally awesome!" Christy's yell quickly followed, and Bjørn wasn't sure if it was Henry's upchucking or the flight that gave her such joy.

Taking pity on the man, Bjørn leveled Annie out and slowed to ease onto the landing spot. Bjørn's oldest brother, Gunnar, waited next to his dogsled team for the next leg of the couple's adventure tour. His arms crossed his chest, and he shook his head in disbelief. Bjørn waved through the windshield as he set the bird down and switched everything off.

"Thanks for flying Rebel Air." Bjørn pulled off his

headset and turned in his seat with a smile. "Hope you enjoyed the adventure."

"Oh, my. That was so much fun," Christy gushed as she leaned forward and clasped his arm. "Thank you for making this flight extra special."

Her lips tweaked as she tilted her head to Henry. Man, this woman had to get rid of that dead weight. She was too adventurous to let Henry ruin her life.

"My pleasure." Bjørn pointed toward Gunnar and the dogs. "The next leg might not have as many thrills, but the company is a lot cuter. The dogs, not the knucklehead brother of mine."

She grabbed her stuff and left the helicopter, not waiting for Henry to follow. Bjørn didn't see their relationship lasting much longer. He extended the lidded trash can he kept stashed toward Henry, who tossed the bag in with a huff and exited without a word. Bjørn saluted to Gunnar, then fired Annie back up. As far as tours went, Henry aside, Bjørn's future was off to a soaring start.

Sadie Wilde tightened her ponytail and yanked the cuffs of her long-sleeved T-shirt down, making sure the fabric covered her scars. She turned one way, then the other in the tiny mirror mounted above the utility sink the teeny bathroom sported. The only other thing in the room was a metal cupboard from the last century hanging over the toilet that they'd painted a cheery teal to hide its age.

Leaning closer to check the reflection of her face, her heart sank into her gut, making it tumble like three week old puppies. Should she have let her sister Violet do her makeup like she'd begged? Would Sadie look washed out for the camera with her typical swipe of mascara and tinted lip balm?

"Who cares?" Sadie rolled her eyes, then stared herself down in the mirror. "Keep it together, Sade. This is important to the kennel. It could be the break we need to rock it. No one else can do this like you. You're the face of North STAR Kennel. You've got this."

"Talking to yourself again?" Denali Wilde, Sadie's best friend and cousin, spoke from where she leaned against the doorjamb, making Sadie jump and whack her head on the cupboard.

"Ouch." She cringed as she rubbed the side of her head and glared at Denali, who had doubled over with laughter. "Not that funny."

"Are you kidding me?" Denali stood up, wiping her finger under her watering eyes. "First you stand there talking to yourself, then you fling your head right into the cabinet." She sighed. "I wish I'd caught that on video. We could have Violet put it on our YouTube channel under behind-the-scenes or something."

"Har. Har. Chuck it up, Buttercup." Sadie leaned against the sink. "I don't remember you volunteering to be interviewed by Nature Channel. If I remember right, your exact words were 'I'll be in front of the camera when penguins fly to Alaska and take up residence.'"

Denali's lips tweaked up on one side of her face. It was good to see her smile and to hear her laugh. After Denali's high school boyfriend had left her pregnant after graduation to chase his hockey dreams of fame, Sadie's cousin had lost her sparkle. Being a single mom would do that. Make one weary and hesitant. Not that they all didn't adore Sawyer and wouldn't do anything for the spunky eleven-year-old.

Denali had wanted to put Sawyer first in everything, though, barely dating anyone the last eleven years. She was tenacious like that, too willing to go down with her lonely ship, even with lifeboats poised and ready. It was a horrible trait when it came to her not opening her caring heart to possibilities for love, but an amazing one when it came to business partners. Though Denali said she wouldn't go in front of the camera, if it meant the business succeeded, she'd be there with her favorite lipstick on.

Sadie cocked her head to the side. Maybe she should let Denali spruce up her makeup? Except for the lips, she was more subtle in her style than Violet was.

"Guys, we have a problem." Aurora, Denali's sister and the oldest of the four of them, rushed up behind Denali. "Reggie is sick."

"What do you mean, sick?" Sadie followed them out to the kennel's fenced yard where the dogs hung out.

They'd just gotten Reggie from his owner a week before for SAR training. The beagle showed real promise of being a much-needed asset to Search and Rescue. Sadie had begged her friend from Anchorage to let her train the energetic dog. If something had happened under her watch, she'd never hear the end of it.

"He's throwing up and has the runs." Aurora held the door open for Sadie and Denali, a look of horror on her face.

While Rory loved the dogs and North STAR Kennel's mission, she stayed in the office. They would lose the business without her organizational and money skills. It worked out great for Sadie, who hated anything indoors or math related, even if it meant she had little in common with Rory.

"What if it's parvo?" Rory whispered, like she worried the dogs would hear.

Dread slid under Sadie's skin, chilling her like glacial runoff. If Reggie had parvo, that could ruin them. Sadie's wire-haired pointing griffon, Coco, the matron of their SAR breeding plan, had just popped out her first litter. If they got sick, not only could North STAR lose puppies, but they'd lose the precious funds that litter would bring them.

"Have you called the vet?" Sadie snapped as she raced across the yard to the large shaded kennel Reggie was in.

"Yeah. Mark's on his way." For not being too involved in the training, Rory couldn't stand seeing the animals sick. It was a good thing the local vet was Rory's long-time friend and had a major crush on Rory, even if she didn't see it. "I locked the other dogs in their kennels too, just in case."

She scanned the yard like a dangerous animal waited to pounce. If it was parvo, Rory's freak out wasn't far from the truth. Parvo could wipe out their kennel, both in dogs' lives and in money.

"Good idea." Sadie stepped up to Reggie's enclosure to go in, but got pulled back.

"You can't go in there." Denali tugged Sadie further away. "The people from Nature Channel will be here any minute. You can't go in there then handle the puppies."

Sadie swallowed and looked at Reggie prone on the other side of the chain-link fencing. She couldn't leave him to suffer, but they also needed this break. If she handled him or even stepped on something contaminated as she'd crossed the yard, then brought it into the puppies area, all the puppies could catch it. She should just call her contact and reschedule.

She sighed. "I'll call Drew."

"No, you won't." Denali shook her head, crossing her arms. "The filming crew is leaving tomorrow. We can take care of this. You go do that interview."

"But—"

"No buts, Sadie." Rory pulled Sadie back toward the building. "We need the exposure Nature will give. Mark said he'll bring a test, and we'll know within fifteen minutes if its parvo."

How could she possibly just leave Reggie without making sure he was okay? She stood staring at the poor, sick dog, her heart pounding in her throat like a drum. Taking a deep breath, she turned toward the building. Her cousins were right. Sadie couldn't be in both places, and it would be better for the puppies if someone stayed clear until they figured out what was wrong. Sadie slipped off her sandals at the door, not willing to track anything in, and went to scrub her hands. She couldn't risk bringing any of it to the pups.

"Hello, Sadie?" Drew's Australian accent floated to her, and she quickly dried her hands.

She entered the big training room, a sweat breaking out at the sight of the cameramen and equipment being lugged in. She shook off the nerves. It wasn't like she had a shy bone in her body, unless it came to her ugly scars covering her forearms and marring her collarbone. She loved meeting new people and having fun. She'd just pretend the cameras were the gateway to a ton of new friends.

"Hey, Drew." She smiled as she crossed to him and shook his hand. "Are you ready to see what it takes to make super dogs?"

"I'm more than ready." Drew rubbed his hands together. His bright blue eyes—that probably made his viewers go crazy—sparkled at her. "As soon as the crew gets set up, I'd like to start with a few questions about what you ladies do here at North STAR and then you can show us the puppies."

"Perfect." She watched Mark pass in front of the window as he headed to the backyard.

Drew's chuckle snapped her attention back to him. "Is it a requirement for me to go barefoot?" His eyebrow lifted, and his gaze trailed to her toes.

"No." She wiggled her feet. "We just have a sick dog out back, and I didn't want to track anything in if its something that's contagious."

"Oh, no." Concern splashed across his face. "Do you need to be out there? Is there anything we can do to help?" He glanced at his watch. "We could come back in an hour or so."

She knew there was a reason she liked Drew so much. Not only did he love animals, but his consideration and easy-going personality make him fun to be around. He'd just given her a chance to take care of Reggie.

What if it was parvo, and then she couldn't be with the puppies? Her sister Violet could do the interview, but she was so flighty, she'd probably mess up the entire thing. No, Sadie had to trust that her cousins and Mark could take care of Reggie. Sadie would get the interview done with, then assess the situation.

"No, it's fine." Sadie turned back to Drew, determined to make this opportunity benefit North STAR. "Denali and Rory are out there with the vet. I'd just be in the way."

"Denali's here?" Drew leaned to peer out the window.

Sadie nodded, stifling her smile. So the handsome Aussie had the hots for Denali? Too bad he had to leave the next day, otherwise she'd nudge him on. Though, maybe a date with a nice guy with no chance of it going further was just what Denali needed. Sadie's eyebrow lifted as a plan formed. With the right focus and charm, she'd get this interview done, check on Reggie, and have Denali a dinner date within the next hour.

Chapter Two

"I REALLY APPRECIATE YOU HELPING OUT." Will Wilde, head of the search and rescue team in Seward, threw his pack into the helicopter and stepped back next to Bjørn to let the three SAR members climb in. "Having a chopper here in Seward willing to go out on missions could mean life or death for some of these cases."

"Annie's primary purpose is to help others." Bjørn patted his chopper's side as a calm settled into his bones.

His business plan might be built around tourism, but he had always written on the top of every scrap of paper: "People first. Money second." It was why he'd gone with the versatile, stripped-down cabin that seats could be added to as needed rather than the plush, private-transport package. To him, helping search and rescue would be top priority, even if it meant cancelling a tour. He could always find ways to make money, but someone dying because he wouldn't help would haunt him for life.

"You a Night Stalker?" Will pointed to the 160th SOAR insignia on Annie's nose.

"Yeah." Bjørn sometimes wondered if he'd left the army too soon. He hadn't planned on reenlisting when his tour came up, but not staying now felt like he ran away from the rumors started about him rather than confronting them.

"My cousin John is a lieutenant colonel with the SOAR division." Will flashed Bjørn a smile. "Now that I know I have one of the best chopper pilots in the world at my disposal, you might regret volunteering."

Bjørn half laughed as he forced a smile. If Will looked into Bjørn, what would he find? Would the lies the special forces captain had told to cover how he botched the mission follow Bjørn home?

"This it?" Bjørn tipped his head toward the team waiting in the helicopter.

"Yep." Will opened the door to the copilot's seat and climbed in.

Bjørn stalked around the bird, doing one last preflight check to lower his blood pressure and clear his mind. The demons from his past would not sabotage his present. He'd do his job like he'd always done, putting his entire focus into it. Huffing out one last breath of bitterness, he climbed into his seat.

Slapping on the headset, he powered up Annie, letting the low thump-thump of her rotors calm him even more. He glanced behind him to make sure everyone had buckled in and got a thumbs up from a young woman with bright teal and purple streaks through her hair. Her wide smile spiraled the last of Bjørn's unease out of him, like the air pulled up through the spinning blades.

"Ready to head out?" Bjørn opened the throttle and pulled up on the collective.

"Yep. The Lost Lake area is about fives up the highway." Will wagged his finger in the direction indicated. "The RV park manager called the troopers, concerned when the couple hadn't returned from their hike. She said they'd been all excited about getting to the lake, but never returned yesterday. Troopers found their vehicle at the trailhead."

As Bjørn increased the collective pitch, he depressed the left pedal, countering the torque created by the main rotor. The chopper lifted, and the cyclic became sensitive. Bjørn eased Annie forward. Most people found flying a helicopter more difficult than patting their heads and rubbing their bellies simultaneously, but the controls were just extensions of Bjørn, his hands and feet reacting most times without him having to think.

"Too bad they weren't found on the main trail." Bjørn pointed the nose down the highway and rocketed forward.

"Yeah. Troopers ran the loop before calling us." Will flipped the map in his lap and followed a path with his finger. "The path is marked well, but if someone got adventurous, there are several places to off-shoot."

"All right." Bjørn smiled. "Let's go sightseeing."

Two hours later, and with no luck, the tension in the helicopter had built like Mount Redoubt, ready to blow. It was a quiet pressure, only visible in Will's puffs of frustrated breath and the shifting of the volunteers staring out the windows in the back. Bjørn circled the latest lake they'd searched, hoping one last pass would reveal the missing hikers.

"Dad, remember where that family got lost about ten years ago?" The woman with the brightly colored hair, who couldn't be over twenty, leaned in between the pilot seats and snatched the map from Will's lap. "You all searched for days, yet some extreme backpackers heading for a weeklong camp out finally found them."

"The Smiths." Will grabbed the map and studied it. "We never figured out how they made it that far, though they swore they were just following the trail." He turned in the seat and smiled. "Good job, Violet."

Will pointed on the map, and Bjørn adjusted his direction. Dense, dark green of the towering Sitka spruce trees rushed below him. Hopefully, the tourists weren't stuck in the forest, otherwise they'd never find them from the air.

"So, your daughter does SAR with you?" Bjørn glanced at Will before searching out the window.

"Both of them do." He chuckled. "I passed my addiction down to them."

"Well, what did you expect when you started taking us on calls when we were ten?" Violet laughed over the headset as she pushed on her dad's shoulder from behind.

"Yeah, well, I wanted to teach you responsibility." While Will's tone came across as gruff, his mouth tweaked up on one side. "Didn't know you two would go all in and make a living from it."

"I thought Alaska SAR was all volunteer." The forest opened up to craggy mountain ahead, so Bjørn angled for what looked like a goat path.

"It is. My sister, cousins, and I have started a kennel and training facility for SAR and law-enforcement dogs." Violet gushed from the back. "We just got our first litter of SAR puppies, and, oh my goodness, they are so adorable."

"The girls have talked about it for years, planning

everything out." Will chuckled. "Other girls would play with dolls, but our girls drew up kennel plans and researched best training practices."

"Well, Sadie and the others did. I still played with dolls." Something in Violet's tone said there was more to that story. With six brothers and sisters, Bjørn understood how siblings could get.

"Anyway, the girls started out boarding and training dogs and now have expanded to breeding." Pride stretched from father to daughter, and Bjørn had the urge to call his parents.

Color flashed halfway up the mountainside, yanking Bjørn's attention. "See that flash of blue among the rocks to our eleven?"

Bjørn eased the cyclic forward to get closer as the color shifted and waved. Was it the missing tourists? He checked the gauges. He sure hoped so, otherwise they'd have to head back and fuel up before searching more.

"Definitely two people." Will had the binoculars to his eyes. "One isn't moving from their position on the ground. The other is waving so much she might throw herself off the mountain. She looks like the picture on the driver's license."

Bjørn scanned the mountain up and down. The rocky terrain stretched for thousands of feet up and down from the couple's location. These two had managed to not only get themselves lost, but picked the worse place to get injured. Will waved to the lady, and she collapsed next to her husband. Why hadn't Bjørn installed the winch system the day before when he'd gotten it? If he had, they could just hover above the ledge and haul the people up.

"The man's leg is elevated, probably broke it or

something. His pallor isn't great. We'll definitely have to carry him out." Will sighed as he leaned forward and gazed at the mountain.

"This terrain is nasty." Bjørn pulled up on the collective, and the helicopter climbed. "Let's see if we can find a place to land."

As Bjørn flew back and forth, searching for a place to set down, the boost of hope that had energized him fizzled to a dull throb. He went back over the slope above the couple. The ledge they were on was narrow, like a giant had taken a spoon and scooped the rock away. It wasn't wide enough for him to hover with the door parallel to the ledge. However, the mountain depressed more above where the couple waited. He had an idea, but it would be tricky. He blew out a deep breath and turned to Will.

"Here's what we're going to do. Someone will need to fast rope down and prepare the couple for transport." Bjørn pointed to the rocks above them. "The spot isn't wide enough for me to get in there close with the door, but I can get the front of the skid on that ledge to the right of the couple."

Will nodded, though his eyes widened as he assessed the area Bjørn indicated.

"Once the couple is ready for transport, I'll set the skid down. Whoever is left in here will hook in, run a cable to the ledge across the skid, and we'll guide the couple in." Bjørn had executed missions in similar situations before, but he'd had soldiers trained for the extreme. "The blades will create wind, so you'll need to stay low and compensate for that."

"I'll rappel down with Kemp." Violet clicked from her seat, secured a carabiner into a metal loop in the chopper's roof, and pulled a harness from her pack. "Dad, you and Uncle Joe come across once Bjørn touches down."

"Sure, take the easy route." Will rolled his eyes as he climbed into the back, though his tone only jested. "Why don't you shimmy across the skinny plank?"

"Whine, whine, whine. You've always been a big baby, little brother." Joe joked, and Bjørn wondered how he'd missed the resemblance.

"Three minutes. You were born three minutes earlier than me." Will hooked the rope system to the carabiner, then secured it to his daughter.

Bjørn liked that this family worked together and had fun doing it. It made him miss his own. Sure, Gunner rented a place outside Seward and they hung out all the time, but it had been a while since all the family had gotten together.

"Kemp, you related to these guys too?" Bjørn gazed through the mirror at the younger man in the back getting geared up.

"Nope, sir." Kemp's southern twang was full of laughter. "I'm just here for the show."

"Whatever." Violet swatted her hand at him. "Kemp is the best wilderness medic in Alaska. Not to mention, he just signed a sponsorship with Alley-Oop snowboarding gear. He's the new poster boy of extreme snowboarding. Women flock and fall at his feet. Bjørn, you haven't heard of him?"

Bjørn snorted and shook his head as Kemp's neck and cheeks flamed red. "Can't say I have."

"All right, you two." Will checked the equipment again as Bjørn got the chopper into position. "Remember, slow and steady. I don't want you coming in so hot you bust your legs."

"Okay, Daddy," Violet said with mock exasperation. "Bjørn, we ready?"

"You are clear to go." Bjørn held Annie steady as the two dropped in fast.

"Geesh." Will hissed. "She's gonna be the death of me."

"Glad you got the wild one and not me." Joe chuckled as he pulled the rope back in.

Bjørn snorted as he lowered the helicopter to wait for the go-ahead. Would this be how he and Gunnar were when they had families? The idea spread warmth through his chest, and the need to cross off "find a wife" on his list burned with such heat, he ran his hand over his heart. He might have to carve out some time to get on that, but where would he even start? He wasn't about to troll the bars, and he definitely didn't want a temporary romance with a tourist or seasonal employee. That would be a waste of time. Bjørn shook his head. There'd be time to think about this later. He needed to keep his focus on the rescue, not some elusive future.

When Kemp gave them the thumbs up, Bjørn eased the nose forward, monitoring the rocks above. One clip and he could kill them all. He touched the right skid on the ledge and nodded the all clear. His mouth dried out as Will clipped in and sat on the door's edge. Making sure he held everything steady, Bjørn let out a long, low breath as Will walked across the skid like a pro.

Chapter Three

SADIE PULLED into the library parking lot and jerked her Toyota Land Cruiser into park. She'd completely forgotten about the monthly SAR meeting until Violet called, all worked up about the new volunteer that had flown for their rescue earlier that day. Sadie had wanted to skip the meeting and stay with Reggie. After a negative parvo test and a clear x-ray, Mark was convinced the darn dog had just eaten something that upset his stomach. So, while she'd rather stay at the kennel babying him, especially with the exhausting day she'd had with worrying about him and the interview that had lasted four hours instead of one, she had no excuses not to go.

Violet zipped her car into the next space and popped out with a smile stretched across her face. She'd pulled her hair into two messy buns on the top of her head like a black bear that had gotten into two open paint cans. Sadie loved her sister's sense of individuality, how she wasn't afraid to just be her wild and crazy self. It bled into her art that was bright and, some would say, unconventional, just like her.

"I can't wait for you to meet the helicopter pilot Dad roped in." She leaned against the hood of her car and fanned herself like she would faint. "Swoon worthy to the max."

Sadie rolled her eyes and headed into the library. She never understood Violet's propensity for the dramatic. Maybe it was her expressive, artsy-fartsy way compared to Sadie's own grounded tendencies. Guys weren't just good-looking or nice. They were romance-cover material or the most tenderhearted man ever. She'd flit and flutter like a butterfly from one to the other, landing for a date or two before flapping on to the next.

"I'm serious, Sade. This guy has that whole ex-military, I'll keep you safe and get the job done persona wrapped up in this delicious package of lean muscle and amazing dimples." Violet grabbed onto Sadie's arm and pretended like her knees had buckled. "His name is Bjørn, and I'm telling you, he's like the personification of a Viking warrior."

"So, he's barbaric and grimy, with a beard down to his chest and hair to match?" Sadie asked dryly.

"No, silly." Violet huffed and swatted Sadie on the arm. "He's adventurous and hot as all get-out. Think Thor after his hair was chopped short, but before he turned all fat and despondent."

"So, when's your first date?" How Sadie wished she could find time to date, though the last debacle with the SAR member from Anchorage had left her a little gun-shy. Few men wanted a woman with scars that marred their body like Sadie's did.

"Oh, no. He's just eye-candy, like a statue at the Louvre. Nice to marvel at God's creative genius but by standing behind the red velvet cord, not by exploring the smooth curve of muscles with fingertips."

Sadie threw her head back as a deep laugh burst from her. Where did her sister come up with this stuff? Thank goodness Sadie had come to the meeting. She'd needed a good laugh. She opened the door to the library, heading to the stairs to the meeting room.

"So, dear sister, why is the Viking god statue off limits? Married?" Sadie threaded her fingers through her sister's and swung their hands like they had as children.

"No." Violet shrugged. "He's just too old for me."

"Oh, so he's ancient, like forty or something?" Sadie asked with mock seriousness.

"No, not ancient. He's probably just in his late twenties, early thirties. He was a member of that special ops division Dad's cousin is a part of." Violet pulled her hand from Sadie's, tucked her arm around Sadie's back, and leaned her head on Sadie's shoulder. "You can't be part of that division without being in the military for a long time. I've found men that age are usually looking for something more permanent, and I'm too young to settle down. But you, on the other hand, are getting up there, so he'd be perfect for you."

"Getting up there?" Sadie gasped and pushed her sister away. "I'm only twenty-seven."

"See. That puts you right in his age range." Violet turned and walked backward toward the open doors to the room. "Not yet ancient, but starting to wrinkle around the edges."

"Why you—"

Sadie reached for her sister as she turned with a laugh and dashed into the room. Violet shrieked as

Sadie grabbed the back of her shirt. Wrapping her sister in a headlock, Sadie rubbed Violet's head with a noogie she deserved.

"I'll show you wrinkled." Sadie couldn't contain her smile as Violet laughed and bucked like a moose with its antlers stuck in thick brush.

"Girls." Their dad's exasperated voice lifted over the giggling.

Both Sadie and Violet froze, then looked up at Dad and spoke in unison. "Yeah, Dad?"

They turned to each other and broke out laughing. Dad's sigh could be heard from across the room. His mutter was too low to discern words, but his resignation was clear. Too bad he had had no boys. Even after a quarter of a century, he still wasn't entirely sure what to do with his daughters.

"Can we start the meeting now, or do we need to pull out the boxing gloves?" Dad's question rushed Sadie back to her early teens when she and Violet would argue nonstop. One day, Dad had thrown his hands up, stomped out of the house, and came back in with two pairs of boxing gloves.

"We're good." Sadie rubbed her knuckles on Violet's head one last time, messing up the bear buns and giving her a funny purple tuft in the middle of her head.

Snorts and stifled laughs sounded around the room as Sadie headed to the nearest open seat. Her gaze slammed into the Norse masterpiece that had to be Bjørn, and she swallowed. Violet hadn't exaggerated this time. The man was make-your-feet-stumble good-looking. He had an amused smile on his face as he watched her. His stare heated her core and rushed a hot blush to her cheeks.

Great. Nothing like embarrassing oneself completely in front of the new guy. Not that it mattered, anyway. She pulled on the cuffs of her sleeves to make sure her scars were covered. With her arms the way they were, she'd never have a chance with someone like him. Not that she cared. Not really. With the kennel ramping up, she didn't have time now for anything but focusing on that.

She plopped in the seat and tried to keep her attention on her father. His voice droned on about safety procedures he'd drilled into her over and over again. Her eyes lost focus, and her mind wandered to different ways she could up the difficulty of training for the dogs. She wanted to push them, to test their abilities and learn how she, as the handler, could catch the clues the dogs gave, no matter the situation.

"Last, I'd like to introduce our newest volunteer." Dad motioned for Bjørn to stand up. "Bjørn Rebel just moved back to Alaska after serving in the army for the last thirteen years. He's a decorated soldier, flying in the most elite division, known for their ability to get places most believe unflyable."

The longer Dad talked Bjørn up, the redder Bjørn's ears got. Sadie pressed her lips together to keep from laughing. Good. She wasn't the only one embarrassed.

"Today, not only did he spot the missing tourists, but Bjørn came up with an idea to rescue them I'd never seen anyone actually execute." Dad shook his head in amazement. If Dad was impressed, then Bjørn must be the real deal. Nothing ever impressed her father. "It would've taken us hours to get that couple off of the mountain without his quick thinking. Having him there saved that man's life today."

Man, Dad laid it on thick. Was he really that impressed, or was the speech to make sure the recruit stuck around? Bjørn held up his hands in surrender, then looked behind him in expectation.

"I can't wait to meet this guy you're talking about." Huh. So, the hero's head hadn't inflated with all that hot air Dad had spewed? "I'm just glad I was around to help. I know how precarious life is in these situations. I'm all in, however I can help." He shrugged. "I'll also wrangle my brother to volunteer, though he lives outside of town a bit. He's a retired pararescueman, so this stuff is right up his alley."

Wow. Two siblings with extreme careers? That must have been a competitive family growing up. Maybe his parents were like Sadie's, not letting her and Violet slack or shirk responsibilities. Sadie glanced at Violet, glad they both loved being a part of SAR. Her sister tilted her head toward Bjørn, wiggled her eyebrows, and fanned herself. Sadie rolled her eyes. On second thought, maybe having her sister around wasn't so great.

Bjørn sat back down. His chest heaved like the attention had made it hard for him to breathe. She liked that he didn't have the cocky, I-am-god mentality she'd come up against lately. Okay, that wasn't exactly fair. It was just that one jerk from Anchorage, but he'd left a bitterness she'd have to root out.

Sadie cocked her head to the side as she stared across the room at Bjørn. An idea formed in her mind. Would he be willing to help her with her training? She had been racking her brain to come up with a way that she could acclimate the dogs to flight, but hadn't thought of anything that wouldn't take hours of driving and thousands of dollars. Would her small budget be enough to entice him to fly her and the dogs around?

He glanced across the room, his gaze snagging on hers. His smile built slowly, the left dimple popping out a second before the right. She smiled back before she realized she'd been staring. She bit her bottom lip and turned her attention back to her dad. Shoot. Could the meeting get any more embarrassing? Should she even ask him now that he'd caught her gawking like a lovesick high schooler?

She chanced a peek back at him, thankful that he had bent sideways to talk with Kemp and didn't see her. Dad ended the meeting, and everyone stood to leave or chat. Should she suck it up and ask or sneak out before she added on another layer of humiliation? Any other day, the attention wouldn't have bothered her. So why did Bjørn's presence change that?

Sadie stood and pulled her shoulders back. It didn't change a thing. If she wanted to move North STAR Kennel forward, she'd have to do hard things, like talk the Nordic masterpiece into taking her flying. She just had to remember she wasn't what guys wanted and keep her feet on the ground.

Chapter Four

THE INSTANT BJØRN STOOD, people started introducing themselves. His neck still burned from the way Will had gone on and on about Bjørn's flying. He didn't want everyone thinking he was some narcissistic jerk. Was he confident in his flying? Sure, he could thread his Annie through a needle if he had to. Didn't mean he wanted everyone to think he wasn't just your average Joe.

He especially didn't want the brown-eyed beauty across the room to get the wrong idea about him. Wasn't he just thinking how he needed to work on that getting married item on his to-do list? She wasn't some summer temp or just passing through, either. Her roots were deep in the Alaskan soil.

Here was someone who checked a lot of his boxes when it came to potential wife material. Adventurous? Check. She had to be on some level to volunteer for SAR, which also checked off giving. Family-oriented? Check. He stifled his smile at the memory of her and Violet bursting into the meeting. The Wilde's had a lot in common with the Rebel's. Beautiful? Double check with bright red ink. Her high cheekbones and long neck, along with those dark brown eyes, flashed like a beacon guiding him home. He'd had a hard time keeping his attention off her and on Will's debrief, which wasn't like Bjørn.

He craned his neck above Kemp's head to see if she'd already left. She chatted with her dad on the other side of the room. Good. Or was it? Did he want to get involved with the boss's daughter? Sure, it was all volunteer, but if things didn't work out, it could make SAR uncomfortable.

Geez, Rebel. Get a grip.

He didn't even know her name, and he had a list going of pros and cons? He needed help, like a punch in the face kind of help. Was she even available? She could be married, for all he knew. Though, by the way she was staring at him, he hoped she wasn't. Maybe she'd been staring because his fly was down or something. Bjørn slyly checked just as Violet skipped over.

"You have a little problem with your hair." Kemp pulled on the tuft that stuck out of her buns from her sister's knuckle treatment.

She swatted his hand away. "I like it that way. Gives my style a unique twist."

"I'll say." Kemp crossed his arms as he laughed. Was there something going on between them? "Makes you look like a tufted duck."

Bjørn snorted, then stifled it as Violet's eyes narrowed. She sputtered and threaded her arm through his, turning her back to Kemp, who still laughed.

"Come on, Bjørn. I want to introduce you to my sister." Violet pulled him through the crowd.

She didn't have to pull hard, since that was exactly

where he wanted to go. Being introduced to the sister was a good sign, right? He did a quick recon as they approached. No ring. Another good sign. She smiled at him as Violet led him closer. One more clue for the go ahead.

"Bjørn, this is my sister, Sadie." Violet stepped back and waved her hand between them. "Sadie, this is Bjørn Rebel."

Violet said his name oddly, like there was a secret bouncing between the simple words he wasn't privy to. He ignored how it made the back of his neck warm and stuck out his hand, smiling to cover the discomfort. Sadie's handshake was firm and confident in his, adding another check off the list he hadn't even realized was an itemized element.

"It's really nice to meet you." Sadie pushed her hands into her jeans pockets. "It'll be good to have you on the team."

"Glad to be here." He mirrored her stance by shoving his hands in his vest pockets. "So, your dad was telling me you own a kennel and train service dogs."

Sadie's entire face lit up with pride and excitement. Bjørn's heart thumped in his chest like rotors gearing up for takeoff. His mind blared warning signals of approaching danger. She was even more incredible up close.

"It's amazing." Sadie pulled out her phone, ran her finger across the screen, then flipped it around to a picture of adorable white puppies with brown faces. "We just had our first litter, and they are all already spoken for. Until now, we've just been focusing on the training part, but with these cute little nuggets and our plan to breed our Belgium Malinios next year, we'll be on our way to providing people with dogs specifically bred and trained for protecting and saving lives."

Her enthusiasm infected him with an electric buzz of energy. Was she always this excited, or was it just this jump in their business? They had to be good entrepreneurs for the puppies to be sold.

"So, is your business more focused on the breeding side or training?" Bjørn knew a little about dog breeding with his brothers Gunnar and Tiikâan dog sledding. They'd spent lots of years building the kennel to what it was. Gunnar had even helped while he'd been in the Air Force, having regular calls with Tiikâan to talk dog.

"Oh, no. These puppies won't go to their owners until they're around two years old." Sadie slid through more pictures, turning it to him to show two shaggy-haired, brown dogs. "We'll take the first two years and put them through rigorous training so they're ready to go into the field. The owners will come to the kennel four times a year for training themselves until the dogs are set to go home."

"That's cool." Bjørn wrapped his brain around this concept. "So, you put them through basic, then throw them into advanced individual training."

"Oooh, I like that!" She smiled up at him like he'd just given her the world. "I'm stealing that."

He cleared his parched throat. "Steal away."

"I actually wanted to ask you something." Her cheeks blushed a pretty pink.

Bjørn stepped closer in anticipation. Yes. The answer was yes. It didn't matter what she asked.

"Shoot." He relaxed his shoulders to ease his tension. He didn't want to scare her off by being too eager.

"I'd like to train my older dogs to get used to flying." She shoved her phone in her back pocket, then talked with her hands. "A lot of the rescues we go on require a flight in, and if the dogs aren't trained for that, the stress will make it hard for them to do their jobs. I'm hoping I can get your help with that."

"Yeah, sure." Bjørn nodded. The request wouldn't be hard and would give him more time to get to know her.

"Really? Oh, thank you!" She grabbed his arm just above his elbow and electricity shot through him like a taser, making his muscles flex. "I don't have a huge budget right now, but I could pay you."

Her eyes flicked to her hand still on his arm, then she dropped it. Her fingers flexed beside her. Was she experiencing lingering sparks like he was? She gave him a sheepish smile and shrugged one shoulder, the pink blush deepening.

"You don't have to pay me." Bjørn jumped in to move the conversation along.

"Fuel isn't cheap. I can pay——"

"I'm flying almost daily anyway, getting used to the terrain and weather systems here." Bjørn interrupted her, not wanting her to get the wrong idea. "It'd be nice to have someone to talk to other than myself or Annie."

Actually, he enjoyed being in Annie alone, experiencing the beauty Alaska offered with no pressure from command or the adrenaline missions built in his muscles. He'd loved being a Night Stalker, but the stress had started to take a toll on him. Yet, he'd sacrifice his quiet solitude if it meant he could get to know this fascinating woman more.

"Who's Annie? Is she your wife?" Her color blanched.

"No. No wives or girlfriends. Haven't had either for a long, long time."

Sadie's eyes widened, and she took a small step back. Shoot. What had he just said? His neck heated as realization crashed over him.

"I mean, I've never had a wife, let alone plural." He stumbled over his words like some nervous teenager. "Haven't even had a date in almost a decade." Seriously? Could a hole open up and swallow him, please? "Annie is my chopper." He blurted the last out, closing his eyes to escape his humiliation.

Her low chuckle settled in his gut. He peeked at her with one eye to see just how much damage he'd done. Her lips pressed together, and her eyes sparkled.

"Would you be able to swing by the kennel tomorrow so we can make a plan?" Her watch beeped, and her forehead scrunched when she glanced at it.

"Sure. I'm free all day." Obviously, since he'd just spewed how pathetic his life was.

"I'm usually there at six in the morning until late." She pulled out her phone, messed with the screen, then handed it to him. She'd typed his name in the contact form. "I have no life, boyfriend, or anything else at the moment except the kennel, so it seems we're in the same boat."

Though his mind cheered she was single, he focused on putting his info in. Maybe he hadn't messed up his chance at getting to know her better. When he handed the phone back to her, she held it up and snapped a picture. She giggled low and showed him a goofy picture of him all wide-eyed, like she'd startled him.

"Okay, I'll swing by in the morning." He crossed his arms so he didn't snatch her phone and delete the picture.

"Great. I'll text you directions." She reached out for a handshake. Her smile was warm, and her palm sparked against his own. "I look forward to chatting with you more." She pulled away and pointed with her thumb over her shoulder. "I hate to run, but I have a sick dog I have to check on before I go home."

"Is it serious?" He knew how quickly a dog could turn south.

"No. He just ate something he shouldn't have." She stepped backward, waved big at someone behind him, then gave him one last smile. "See you tomorrow."

"Yep." He rocked on his heels. "Looking forward to it."

She pressed her lips together, then turned and stepped out the door. Was she hiding a smile, or was that a look of concern? She jogged to catch up with someone ahead of her, her cheery voice floating back to Bjørn. He blew out a long breath. What the heck just happened? He'd come to the meeting looking to volunteer, never expecting he'd offer so much.

Chapter Five

SADIE TRUDGED in from training the dogs in the backyard with Reggie nipping at her heels. Her energy
dragged, and she needed another cup of coffee. She
hadn't been able to sleep so had come in around four to
check on him. She had told the plucky beagle it was all
his fault she'd tossed and turned all night. He'd just
huffed and looked at her like she was full of it. She was,
of course, and the fact that the dog called her out had
her worried.

No matter how many times she'd lain in bed, telling
herself she couldn't get all worked up about Bjørn, her
stinking, hormone-infused mind wouldn't let it rest.
She'd replayed the meeting and their talk over and over
until her brain had decided she wanted it on a constant
loop. She'd finally been able to fall asleep on the kennel's
couch sometime after six, only to have punctual Aurora
scuttling in at eight to crunch numbers or whatever it
was she did as she typed away on her computer all day.

To add to Sadie's lack of sleep, she'd had the lovely
job of digging through all of Reggie's poop from the

night. Thankfully, she'd found what appeared to be a plastic piece from a toy. With a few days of chicken and rice, Reggie's system should be back to normal. She eyed him at her feet, her face scrunching up in doubt. Unless he swallowed something else he shouldn't have.

Her stomach growled, and she pressed her hand to it as she glanced at the clock. How was it already ten? She'd have to get more than coffee. Maybe she'd run out and grab something at Rez Art. She turned to head back to the yard to ask the others if they wanted something when the front door opened. The howl of a wolf that was the kennel's bell sounded, and Bjørn walked in.

The sun haloed his body like some saint. A robin belted out a song of greeting like Bjørn had paid the thing to make his entrance grand. Not that he needed musical accompaniment or backlighting. Sadie bet he walked into any space and the world stopped for a moment to gawk. Did that make the gravity around him different? She bet it did, because she was rooted to the spot, staring.

"Is this a good time?" Bjørn closed the door with his foot, bringing her attention to the cup carriers and the paper bag clutched in his hands.

"Yeah." She hurried forward and reached for one carrier. "Let me help you."

The Rez Art logo on the cups had her mouth watering and her stomach hollering to fill it. She really should've grabbed a granola bar or something hours ago. The smell of lemon, lavender, and sweet coffee hit her, and her stomach groaned so loud it shook.

Bjørn's smile stretched across his face, his dimples caving in on his cheeks. "You have a bear in there?" His low chuckle filled her with warmth, like she'd chugged a rich cup of Mexican mocha.

"Maybe," she quipped back as she took the carrier and headed to the small kitchen area. "More like time got away from me. I can't believe you stopped at Rez." She turned and cocked an eyebrow. "Are you a mind reader or something? I literally was just going there to grab breakfast."

"Nope, just wanted a coffee and figured I'd bring enough for everyone." He set the other carrier and bag down.

"Well, you're my hero."

Refusing to look at him, she snatched the bag, breathed in the buttery goodness, and pulled out her favorite lavender lemon scone. She took a big bite. Zesty citrus and flowers zipped along her tongue, and she closed her eyes with a sigh. How could the Bell Tower Bakery in the Resurrect Art Coffee House make flour and butter taste like angels made them?

"So good," she spoke around the bite.

"The barista said it was your favorite." Bjørn's words popped her eyes opened.

He'd asked about her? Was that just him being considerate, or did it mean more? She mentally shook herself. She'd been over it a thousand times the night before. It didn't matter how attractive or nice Bjørn was. Men like him would never want someone scarred like her. She swallowed the scone past the lump in her throat.

"Thanks, but you didn't have to." She grabbed the to-go cup he extended to her and took a tentative sip. The rich, smooth cinnamon and chocolate of the

Mexican mocha coated her mouth, giving her brain the jolt of caffeine needed to bring her back to reality.

"I didn't mind." He shrugged and took a bite of his own scone. His eyebrows winged up in surprise as he pulled it away from his mouth to look at it. "Wow. This is amazing."

"Right?" Sadie let his easy manner settle her more.

Was he always this comfortable to be around? She hoped so. Handsome or not, he seemed like he'd be a good friend.

"Are your sister and cousins here?" He motioned to the rest of the cups. "The barista made their favorites too."

Sadie shook her head in both amazement and teasing. "I don't think we need to share."

"No? You don't like to share?" His eyes danced with a smile as he stared at her while he took a slow drink.

"I don't mind sharing." She took another bite, then used the scone to point at the bag. "We could always hide the bag, though. I mean, they'd still have the fantastic coffee, and the girls would never know."

"Never know what?" Denali asked from behind her.

Sadie puffed out a surprised breath, spraying scone crumbs onto her shirt. Bjørn took another drink to hide his laugh. Man, those dimples of his were killers. She brushed off her shirt, put her finger to her mouth to shush him, and turned to her family.

"Hey, Bjørn brought breakfast." She stepped back even with him while displaying the goods with her hand dramatically, like a game show assistant.

"Oh, pastries!" Violet bounced on her toes as she peeked into the bag and pulled out a muffin. "You sure know the way to a girl's heart."

"Really? I'll have to remember that." He peeked at Sadie before tipping his cup to the counter. "Truth is, I was out of coffee at home and didn't want to be rude."

"Feel free to not be rude any time you want." Violet grabbed the cup with her name on it and took a long drink. "Ah, sweet vanilla, how I needed you."

Denali pulled a scone out, and her brow wrinkled as she squinted at Sadie. "You weren't going to tell us about what, exactly? The scones or the entire bag?"

"I don't know what you're talking about." Sadie spoke around her bite as she licked her fingers.

"Maybe she's talking about your addiction to these scones." Aurora pushed up her glasses as she located her cup. "Or she could be referring to that time the mayor brought celebratory cookies, and you hid them in the cupboard with the medical supplies."

"You guys don't even like peanut butter cookies." Sadie sputtered through her giggles, remembering the shocked look on Denali's face as the Tupperware full of cookies had tumbled from the cabinet.

"No, you keep telling yourself we don't like peanut butter so you don't feel guilty eating them all." Denali waved the last lemon lavender scone in the air. "Kind of like you wanted to hide these gems."

Sadie lunged for the pastry, but Denali pulled it out of the way. Reggie yipped a joyful bark and circled between them, probably hoping the scone would drop. Bjørn tipped his head back and busted out laughing. All the women froze like they were caribou that just realized a wolf was in their midst. Sadie turned to find him leaning against the counter, his gaze darting between her, Violet, Denali, and Aurora.

"Don't mind me." He popped the last of his scone in

his mouth.

"Sorry." Sadie wiped her hands on her jeans. "We sometimes forget not everyone is family around here."

"Don't apologize. I have six siblings." He waved his cup toward them. "All this is like home."

Six siblings? Were they all overachievers like Bjørn and his pararescueman brother? She pointed to Denali.

"Bjørn, these are my cousins Denali and Aurora, and this cute guy is Reggie." Sadie bent down to pet Reggie and calm him down. "Denali's focus is the law enforcement service dogs."

"And I'm the computer nerd." Aurora lifted her cup. "I'm totally okay with letting these three do the whole adventure thing."

"It's nice to meet you all." Bjørn gazed around the building. "It's pretty incredible you're doing this. Transforming this place couldn't have been easy."

Sadie followed his gaze and wondered what he saw. The half-century-old house had taken a lot of elbow grease and paint to make it presentable. They'd ripped out walls to bedrooms to make the main room larger. They'd had to replace all the flooring, so it'd be easy to clean. She loved the bright colors and amazing mural Violet had painted on the wall. This place was home more than her cabin she shared with Denali and her son was, but what did others see when they visited?

"This place is amazing." Bjørn whistled low. "Did you have to renovate yourself?"

"Yeah, except for the electrical and plumbing." Sadie toned down her excitement and pride his words had pushed to the surface. "It was a real mess, but we've been able to make it work. Would you like a tour? I was about to give the puppies their Super Dog training. You can help if you want."

Okay, Sadie. Stop talking and let the guy answer.

"Super Dog, huh?" He straightened to follow her. "If you're teaching them to fly, why do you need me?"

"It's early cognitive training. I definitely still need you." Oh, dear Lord. Had she really just said that?

She waved him to follow her as she turned to hide the heat rising up her neck. Violet tucked her head down, her snicker still audible. Violet had caused Sadie's brain to have this meltdown with her Norse god comments and her suggestion that Sadie and Bjørn would be perfect together. If her sister had kept her mouth shut, Sadie would just view him as another one of the guys.

She peeked back, deciding his profile definitely was Louvre worthy. Plus, he delivered baked goods and coffee on a whim. She turned forward and blew out a breath that caused her lips to flutter together. Who was she kidding? Bjørn Rebel was the epitome of a heart-throb. That didn't mean she had to act on her attraction, especially if she wanted to keep her own heart safe from snapping like a glacier calving into the ocean.

Chapter Six

BJØRN GRABBED the last puppy to run it through the Super Dog moves. He held it under its front legs so its body hung for three seconds, turned the pup upside down, cradled it against him on its back like a baby, then placed it on the cold, damp towel. The puppy yipped the entire time, and Coco, the puppy's mom, kept trying to push her way to save her baby.

"I'm not sure why this is supposed to make them smarter." Bjørn took the puppy and set it in the whelping box with its siblings. "Theoretically, I get it. The military put me through intense training, so I understand how it can make you a stronger person, both physically and mentally. You said they are only six days old. Why put these puppies through this now? Why not wait until they're older?"

Sadie sat back on her heels, her face lighting up with excitement. "It has something to do with the electrical synapses in the brain."

She spoke wildly with her hands, making motions with her fingers like something bounced between each hand. He liked how animated she got when she talked. He'd have to think of things to ask so he could watch her more.

"During this rapid growth phase between day three and sixteen there's like a crazy amount of activity happening in the brain. You know your brain has all these electrical connections, kind of like a web. Doing these exercises creates just enough stress to build more connections." She stared into the box where the puppies nursed, a soft smile on her face. "It's amazing, really. If you do more than three to five seconds for each exercise or do it more than once a day, it's too much on the dog and breaks them somehow. Yet, just this circuit of moves that take less than a minute a pup makes dogs that are not only smarter but are more calm under stress with healthier immune systems."

Bjørn knew all about the breaking point. Isn't that what the military pushed those enlisted toward, especially the ones like him who wanted the crazy path of special ops? Constantly seeing just how far a soldier would let pain and mental anguish go before giving up. It was what had honed him into one of the best pilots in the Night Stalkers. He watched the puppies crawl on their mom. If it was so beneficial for dogs, had any research been done on people?

"Would something like this work on human babies?" He turned back to Sadie.

"I haven't done a lot of research into it since I don't have any babies." She shrugged and pushed against the wooden box to stand. "From what I've read, we are a lot like the puppies. It's why giving babies affection, talking to them, and playing with them is so important, even when they are only eating, sleeping, and pooping machines. It's also why babies that are neglected have so many cognitive and social problems. The synapses weren't properly connected."

Her mouth pulled down and her forehead scrunched in concern, like she wanted to find all those poor babies and bring them to her kennel to take care of. Bjørn shook his head at his thoughts and stood. He didn't have a clue what she was thinking. What he knew was that his brain had kind of frozen for a second while she talked about babies, and veered off course, wondering what her babies would look like.

"You'll have to make a list for me." He cleared his throat, needing to get his mind back on track.

"A list?" She headed toward the sink and washed her hands.

"Yeah, a list of how you do this Super Dog training." He pumped soap on his own hands and stood next to her at the sink. "My brother, Gunnar, mushes. He's training for the Yukon Quest and Iditarod this winter. I bet this would work for his dogs too."

"Yeah, sure." She shrugged and stuck her hands under the water. "I guess I can make a list."

The humor in her voice didn't escape him. Not everyone needed lists like he did, but it kept him organized, knowing what needed done next. He pushed her hands out of the way to rinse his off, splashing her when he finished. She laughed, tossed the towel at him, then quickly yanked her sleeves down over her wrists.

"So, speaking of lists." He hung the towel on the hook in the wall, then leaned against the sink. "Do you have a plan for how you want to do this flight training?"

"Yeah, sure. Kind of." She bit the side of her bottom lip, her eyes full of amusement. "Though, I don't have anything formal written up. Nothing but a bunch of scribbles."

"Let's see what you've got." He could always make an action plan later.

She led him back to the front room and sat on the couch, pulling the coffee table closer. The sunlight filtered through the window and made the red in her brown hair pop. She pushed her long ponytail over her shoulder, then shifted papers on the table. How long was it when she let it down? She glanced up at him and tipped her head to the couch next to her.

"I won't bite. Unless you have another lemon scone hiding in your pocket." Her head shook in mock serious-ness. "If that's the case, I can't be held responsible for what might happen."

"Duly noted. Don't keep snacks with me unless I'm prepared to share." He circled the table and sat down next to her. "And if I really want bonus points, I'm thinking peanut butter or lemon would work."

"Smart man." She whistled for Rowdy, her male, wire-haired, pointing griffon—and the puppies' father—who had just pushed through the doggie door. "So, here's my plan: I think we start with Rowdy here, so I only have to focus on one dog at a time. He's already skilled at search and rescue. Getting him acclimated to flying will make him even more beneficial to the team." She rubbed behind his ear with one hand and pointed at a map on the table with another. "I was studying the area this morning and picked spots that would be good tourist drops, that way you can get familiar with places you could advertise as destinations, either fly-in camp-ing, backpacking, or day picnic-type trips."

As he stared at her, a heat unfurled in his chest at her

thoughtfulness. He hadn't really thought about turning this into a benefit for his business, but she had. He figured it would accustom him to the land for SAR. That alone would be worth taking her out. Not only that, but she'd thought of a part of his business that he'd not slated for further down the line. He'd be able to increase his business a lot sooner than he had written on his timeline.

"Thanks, Sadie." He turned his attention to the maps. "I wanted to offer those kinds of services, eventually. This will help me do it sooner than I planned."

"You scratch my back. I scratch yours." She shrugged. "I want us both to get something out of this, and not just that you have someone to talk to."

He knew it was just a saying, but the phrase had his mind wandering. His gaze lingered on the shell of her ear that was the perfect size, and the sway of her hair as she leaned over the map. He hadn't felt this much attraction to someone in a long time, and he definitely hadn't been this distracted. Was it just the drive to cross the next thing off that stupid list of his? Was the intel his brain fired through him reliable? This development needed analysis before he fired his engines and launched a mission he wasn't prepared for.

He tore his gaze from her and scooted toward the table. "So, where do you want to go first?"

"Well, there are a coup—"

The door opened with a howl. He'd have to ask her where they bought that bell. If he could install it without Gunnar knowing, it'd be a great joke. One Bjørn could catch on video. A man walked in, took off his sunglasses, and scanned the room.

Sadie did a double take. "Drew, what are you doing here? I thought your flight was this morning."

"Sadie, I have the most amazing news." He crossed to the couch and pulled her up. "Are the others here?"

Sadie pulled her sleeves down, then patted him on the arm. "Sure, let me go get them." She turned to Bjørn, her teeth clenched and her face scrunched in apology. "I'll be right back."

"No worries. Take your time." He waved her off.

She rushed out of the room to the back.

"Sorry to interrupt, man." Drew outstretched his hand toward Bjørn. "Drew Wilder."

"It's not a problem." Bjørn shook Drew's hand, trying to place where he knew the name from. "Bjørn Rebel."

Sadie returned with her sister and cousins. They all held varying expressions of surprise and concern. Drew's shoulders relaxed as he stepped toward them.

"Did the Nature Channel not like the interview?" Denali asked, her hands wringing in front of her.

The Nature Channel had interviewed them? That's where Bjørn knew Drew from. He starred in that extreme wild animal show that travelled to the craziest places in the world. What was he doing interviewing at a kennel?

"No. I mean, they loved it." He grabbed her hands in both of his, then let go quickly. "They want us to do an entire series."

"What?" Violet gasped, her hands going to her cheeks.

"What do you mean, series?" Denali crossed arms over her chest, her eyes narrowing.

"Nature loves the idea of a group of amazing

women defying odds and attacking the Alaskan wilderness head-on." Drew motioned between the ladies as the excitement grew in his voice.

Aurora snorted while Denali rolled her eyes. Bjørn cocked his head as he watched them. Sadie just stared, not saying a word. She chewed on her index finger's knuckle, while her other hand held her elbow. Calculations churned in her brain, and he wished he knew her well enough to tell what she was thinking.

"We aren't doing anything that every other woman and man in Alaska aren't doing as well." Denali shook her head. "It's called life. It's no different from anywhere else."

"Sure, but viewers are obsessed with Alaska." Drew gestured around the room with his hand. "With you ladies being gorgeous *and* adventurous, people will jump on this like a wolf pack on a downed caribou."

Bjørn sat back on the couch as unease slithered along his skin. He wasn't sure he liked the idea of a million people gawking at Sadie and her family. He also had no say in the matter. He bit the inside of his cheek to keep his mouth shut.

"I'm not sure I enjoy being referred to as prey." Denali narrowed her eyes, her arms tightening around her front. "And I definitely don't want to be forced to stage things for some audience like a joke. I mean, there's not much *real* Alaska in those shows everyone is so obsessed with."

"We wouldn't film ours that way." Drew held up his hands like he was calming the wolves he'd just spoken about. "I'd make sure that everything we did was authentic. The last thing I'd want is to make you look bad or uncomfortable."

"Too late for that," Denali muttered.

If Bjørn heard it sitting five feet away, Drew definitely heard it. Bjørn snorted, then rubbed his mouth to cover his amusement. Drew had an uphill battle with this group. From what Bjørn could tell, everything they did benefited others. Showcasing for a television show didn't fall in line with that.

"How would this work exactly? What are you wanting to film?" Sadie spoke for the first time, turning everyone's eyes to her.

Denali's mouth popped open. Her face held an expression of incredulity, like she couldn't believe that Sadie wanted to consider the idea. Violet bounced on her toes like she wanted to start filming right then. Aurora just pushed her glasses up on her nose and cocked her head at Sadie.

"Me and two other cameramen would stick around for a month or two and film what you all do." Drew shrugged like it was no big deal, but his shoulders bunched. "Nature will pay a generous amount upfront, then you'll receive royalties when the show produces above and beyond that initial payment."

"Just film us throughout the day? How is that going to be TV worthy?" Sadie motioned with her hand. "It's not always hopping fun around here."

"That's all right. The mundane interests people as much as the wild." Drew shoved his hands in to his pockets.

"How much is generous?" Aurora crossed her arms in a mirror of her sister.

"I mean, you'll have to negotiate, which I suggest you do, but they are already prepared to offer six figures." Drew dropped the amount like a well-placed grenade, making even Bjørn's heart pound. "Each."

Well played. He liked this guy. While Bjørn didn't know the kennel's financial status, that amount of money could make any business secure for many years. If the ladies capitalized on the opportunity, it would generate income well after they stopped filming. Shoot, he'd do back flips and sing karaoke for that kind of money.

"But what would they film? It's not like what we do is all that exciting." Denali waved her arms around.

Why wouldn't she want to make a guaranteed income like what Drew suggested? If the series tanked or the network decided not to air it, the ladies would still have the initial payment. Violet wrapped her arm around Denali's waist and squeezed.

"Denali, I know you didn't want to be in front of the camera, but this isn't something we can pass up." Sadie dropped her arms and motioned to the backyard. "Think about what we could do with the dogs, what we could do for the community. We wouldn't have to wait to expand."

"If we played it right, we could make even more on merchandising, not to mention the fact that the exposure could bring us more clients." Aurora's matter-of-fact tone said the discussion was over, but Denali shook her head.

"It could also backfire." She hugged herself tight again. "We aren't that entertaining."

Bjørn knew that wasn't the truth. He'd only been around the family for a few hours but already had been drawn in. They wouldn't have a hard time getting viewers.

"There's plenty of room in the chopper for a camera or two." The words tumbled out of Bjørn's mouth, and part of him wished he could snatch them from the air and shove them back in. He had looked forward to time alone with Sadie to get to know her.

Everyone turned to him like they'd forgotten he was even there. Bjørn smirked as he stood and joined them. He would've forgotten, too, if that kind of money was being tossed around.

"We were already planning training trips for your search and rescue dogs." Bjørn pointed to the coffee table. "If you filmed those first, you'd have time to figure out how you wanted to do the law enforcement side of the business."

He kept his gaze on the ladies. He wanted them to know he was doing this for them, not the network or even Drew. If his help could ease some of Denali's hesitance, then he'd take Sadie and her dogs out every day for a month straight if he had to. He held Sadie's gaze, her brown eyes thoughtful.

"That could work." She turned to Drew. "Would the network pay for fuel?"

"Yep." Drew turned to Bjørn, his mouth turned up on one side in a thankful smile.

Bjørn gave the man a small shake of the head in warning. Don't get too cocky, yet. Bjørn was pretty sure the Wilde women were an all-or-nothing type of family. If Denali didn't give in, the others would respect that, even though they'd be disappointed.

"If Bjørn's a regular on the show, would he get paid for that as well?" Sadie crossed her arms, her face steely in a challenge.

"Yeah." Drew shrugged. "I don't know specifics, but usually others are paid for each second on air."

"So, if he's on the screen for ten minutes of an episode, he'd be paid six hundred seconds?" Aurora asked.

"That's right." Drew nodded.

"Will you help us make sure he gets a premium rate and that his business is showcased as well?" Sadie asked, and Bjørn opened his mouth to protest, only to snap it shut at her quick glare.

Sadie lifted her eyebrow at Drew, her eyes flicking to Denali, who had her fingers pressed along her eyebrows and was shaking her head. Drew's gaze followed, his face softening a bit before turning back to Sadie.

"I'll help however I can to make this the most beneficial to everyone." Drew's conviction was so strong, Bjørn wondered just how far Drew would go to keep his word.

Sadie stifled a smile, then winked at Bjørn. Beautiful, smart, *and* cunning? Bjørn's attraction lifted from safe ground, soaring to new levels that gave him vertigo and made his head spin. His heart raced as he watched Sadie launch into ideas, her hands waving as she talked. He was such a goner. Excitement built in her voice, and she touched his arm, including him in her plan. The familiar rush of adrenaline that only came when he flew a mission coursed through him. Sadie was an adventure he hadn't planned for, but it was one he could dive full speed into.

Chapter Seven

SADIE PULLED up next to Bjørn's helicopter at the far end of the Seward Airport chopper parking. Gray clouds hung low on the mountains across the bay, pushing down on her. Why couldn't it be bright and sunny instead of gloomy? Maybe then she wouldn't be so nervous, her body leaking cold sweat like a faucet, with the stress of the upcoming training. They weren't even leaving the airport, but the thought of failing had kept her up all night long.

Rowdy sat in the passenger seat, looking out the window in expectation. His tail wagged as his head swiveled from side to side as he took in the action. Drew and his cameramen pulled things from their rental SUV, opening cases of equipment. She was half hoping they'd call to reschedule, say that something more exciting came up, like a herd of moose dancing the cha-cha in downtown Anchorage.

Sadie searched for Bjørn but didn't see him. She still couldn't believe he'd jumped in when he had. She hadn't thought she could talk Denali into doing the show, and none of them would have forced her if she'd insisted. Then Bjørn's suggestion had been enough to give Denali the breathing room she'd needed to realize just how important the opportunity was. Hopefully, Sadie'd find a way to thank Bjørn for his help.

"Come on, Rowdy." Sadie rubbed behind the dog's shaggy ear. "Let's go on an adventure."

He barked a cheerful response and barreled out her door the instant her feet hit the asphalt. He dashed to the crew, sniffing at each of them in greeting. Sadie shivered as the damp air hit her, and she zipped up her jacket and snagged her beanie from the dashboard. So much for looking nice for the camera. Bjørn jumped down from the chopper, and her dog made a fool of himself.

"Rowdy!" Bjørn slapped his knees, and Rowdy's entire body wagged as he rushed to Bjørn. "How are you, buddy?"

Bjørn rubbed Rowdy's side, and the dog's tongue hung out of his mouth in complete bliss. The enthusiasm of the two eased the nerves that zinged along her skin from high-powered electric-fence level to shock-collar level. Reaching into a side pocket of his cargo pants, Bjørn pulled out a tennis ball. Her muscles loosened even more. Not only did he bring baked goods and coffee, but he armed himself with toys for the dog. Sadie shook her head. Did his generosity ever end, or was this all just for show?

"Look what I brought you." Bjørn held the ball high, and Rowdy instantly sat. "Oh, good boy." Bjørn chucked it far into the grass field while Rowdy's body trembled in anticipation. "Go get it."

Rowdy shot off, his legs blurring as he raced to the

ball. Maybe Sadie should go running with him, get some of this energy out that was making her sweaty. Bjørn pushed his sunglasses up onto the top of his head as he strode up to her.

"You ready for this?" His face beamed with excitement, like a kid going to an amusement park.

She shook her head in the negative. "Yes?"

Bjørn chuckled. The low sound tumbled over her head and down her body, causing her to smile. Maybe she had nothing to worry about after all.

"I sense some hesitation in you." Bjørn turned to reward Rowdy, who ran toward them.

"Yeah." She motioned to the network's people. The cameramen already filmed them, and she tensed. "My mind's been telling me all night the reasons this isn't a good idea." She lowered her voice, not sure how well the camera would pick it up. "What if I'm not able to do this? What if the training fails or Rowdy freaks out?"

Bjørn stepped closer and placed his hand on her shoulder. He leaned in, his heat pushing more of the cold away. Confidence replaced his excited expression.

"You've got this." He pitched his voice so only she could hear. "You've done amazing with Rowdy, but even if he freaks out a little, it doesn't mean you've failed. It means you both have an opportunity to improve, to push yourselves. Just keep your head on and forget about the cameras."

"Okay." Her response stuck in her throat in a soft whisper, so she nodded.

"Okay." Bjørn gave her shoulder a squeeze, then bent to take the ball from Rowdy as Drew stepped up.

"Morning," Drew said with a lift of his head. "You ready for this?"

"Absolutely." Sadie shoved her trembling hands in her pockets, and Bjørn shot her a smile. Drew didn't need to know she was so nervous she hadn't been able to eat a thing.

"Great. What I'd like you to do today is just talk me through what it is you're planning, like I'm clueless." Drew motioned to the cameramen following Rowdy as he raced back. "You remember Bo and Craig, right?"

Sure, if her brain wasn't stalled out, she probably would've remembered their names. She gave a tight smile at the men and held her hand up in a wave.

"They're just going to keep rolling the entire time. Try to ignore them, unless they ask a question or tell you to do something." Drew planted his legs wide and hung his arms next to him like he didn't have a care in the world. "Think of me as someone you're training. There's no pressure here. I'll look through the feed before I send it in and cut anything too embarrassing."

"Is that something you normally do?"

"No, but I want to be a man of my word and not give you all any reason to doubt this will be a success." Drew shrugged, but Sadie could tell their trust was important to him.

"Why are you doing this?" Curiosity had branded her since he'd shown back up at the kennel. "Aren't you supposed to be off to the wilds of the world, filming the next adventure? I mean, why were you here in the first place? This kind of show isn't your normal thing."

Drew stared after the dog rolling in the grass. He heaved a loud sigh, then turned his attention to her.

"I never expected my show to get as big as it did. It was just supposed to be a way to save up the funding I needed to do what I really want." He shoved his hands in his front pockets and blew out a laugh. "It kind of took over … everything. It wasn't until I was in the middle of the jungle in South America, so sick I couldn't move, that I finally had a wake-up call. The adventure had gotten old, and my dream finally pushed its way back to the surface."

"What dream?" Sadie asked, a needle of doubt pricking her brain.

"I've always wanted to open a wildlife rehabilitation center." The weariness that had pulled his face low lifted as he looked at her. "I watched a documentary when I was younger about this man who saved eagles here in Alaska, fixed them, then sent them back into the wild to live. It fascinated me, and from that moment on, I wanted to do the same, only by taking in all kinds of animals, not just eagles. But after I graduated from vet school with a mountain of debt, I realized just how hard it'd be to open a facility like I wanted. I was working at a kangaroo rehabilitation center when Nature came in to shoot a piece, and next thing I know, I've got a nice contract and I'm jetting to my first location."

His story pushed at her core, making her break out into a sweat all over again. What if the series had the opposite effect she hoped for? She didn't want to become mired in the success of it if it changed what they'd always planned as their vision. Staring at Rowdy as he bounded to Bjørn, she shook her head. She'd just have to make sure that didn't happen. They'd stay true to their vision or cut the network loose. The resolve eased the nerves and doubt.

"Would your center be in Alaska or back in Australia?" She bit her bottom lip to keep her smile contained.

"Alaska." Drew's quick answer had her smile break free. Had it always been Alaska, or was a certain redheaded cousin of hers to blame for the location? "Actually, I think I've found a place just outside of Seward that is going to work perfectly."

Sadie snorted out a laugh, quickly covering it with a cough.

"What?" Drew flipped his palms up and shrugged.

"Nothing." Sadie couldn't wait to see how this all played out. "I'm glad you're going to be around more."

Sadie whistled to Rowdy as she pulled his leash out of her pocket. Drew's story seemed to flip off the switch to the nerves that had jolted her all night long. With him helping them, he wouldn't let her and her family spiral from their goal like he had. She'd just relax and enjoy this training and her new friends, like the cameras weren't even there.

"You should've seen how amazing Rowdy did." Sadie brushed out Rowdy's coat as she told Denali about the training session. "Bjørn brought a tennis ball with him —had it in his pocket—and Rowdy melted in the guy's hand."

"How did the filming go?" Denali crossed her arms, her teeth worrying her upper lip.

"At first, it was weird having a camera constantly pointing at me." She stood, pulled the bits of grass, seeds, and hair from the brush, and tossed the clump in the trash. "But, honestly, after a while, I completely forgot they were even there. Drew was great at keeping me focused, so I didn't really have time to think about the cameras."

"Yeah, he's smooth like that." Denali huffed and flopped on the grass with her Belgian Malinois, Hank.

"He's a nice guy." Sadie toed her cousin's foot. "You should give him a break. He's going to be around for a while."

"Two months." Denali threw one arm over her face, hiding her eyes in the crook of her elbow, and laid the other hand on Hank's head. "Two months of filming and then he'll be out of our hair, unless the network wants more, then we'll have to put up with him again."

"Actually …" Sadie tossed the brush in the air, drawing out her response to drive Denali crazy with suspense. "He said he might stick around. Guess he likes it here." She smiled as her cousin's mouth dropped open. "Isn't that exciting?"

A mosquito flew into Denali's gaping mouth as Sadie walked away. She chuckled as Denali sputtered and spat behind her. It'd do Denali good to shake up her world a little. Drew seemed a good bet to be someone who could shake just hard enough to get Denali out of the protective bubble she'd put around her, but not hard enough to pop it before she was ready.

"Hey, wait," she called out to Sadie.

"Can't talk now." Sadie waved without looking. "I'm meeting with Bjørn to plan our next training."

"But … but—"

Sadie shouldn't get so much enjoyment from seeing Denali spin, but that Drew had her twirling in the first place encouraged Sadie. Years had passed since Denali had put so much on herself. Sadie was more than ready to have her cousin back, even if getting her to take a second chance at love took some annoying from a certain hot Australian TV star.

Sadie swung her pack filled with maps over her shoulder and skipped down the front porch steps toward her Land Cruiser, her heart lighter than it had been in a long time. She had known that the stress of getting the kennel up and running had weighed on her, but she hadn't realized just how much until that morning. She never imagined they'd be able to change their trajectory so quickly. Some would say it was crazy, putting themselves out there. Crazy was her jam. She loved the excitement and seeing their dreams expand. She just hoped her willingness to go for the wild didn't end up crashing around them all.

She slowed as her dad pulled in next to her vehicle. His thick eyebrows scrunched over his eyes as he looked at her. Great. What did she do wrong now?

"Good. You're here." Dad stood from the car and leaned against the roof.

"I was just heading out to meet Bjørn to figure out our next training session." Sadie twirled her keys on her finger, trying not to let her impatience show.

"That's why I've come." His forehead furrowed even deeper. "I just got off the phone with John, and I don't think you should train with Bjørn anymore."

"What?" Sadie's keys slipped off her finger and dropped to the asphalt. "You've got to be joking."

"Now, listen." Dad held up both palms on the roof to stop her. "John said there were questions swirling around one of Bjørn's last missions. He's going to dig into it, but he said to proceed with caution with Rebel."

"Dad, just the other day you were proclaiming him a superhero." Sadie stepped up to her dad's car.

"I never said that." He scoffed.

"Now you're telling me to stay clear?" Sadie waved her hands around. "What, are you not going to accept his help if a SAR call comes in?"

"No, that's different." He speared his fingers through his hair.

"Different? Really?" She shook her head. "So, you trust him in a life and death situation, but just not when it's a training run? How exactly does that work?"

"Because one is a necessity, and the other is frivolity." He pushed from the car and paced toward the trunk and back.

"So, improving my business and training dogs to handle intense situations is frivolous?" Sadie's neck heated as her anger and frustration rose.

"That's not what I meant." Dad turned to her, determination in his eyes.

"Just what exactly did Bjørn do that has you so concerned?" She crossed her arms over her chest to control her hands.

"He didn't land where he was supposed to, and it cost men their lives." He exploded, his loud voice jolting her head back.

Her chest heaved as his words set in. Could it be true? She knew little about special ops and military missions, but it didn't seem like something Bjørn would do. Since she'd met him, he'd done everything he could to help others. Her own father had exclaimed about how he'd never seen as proficient flying as what Bjørn did to rescue the stranded couple.

Then again, Dad's cousin John was a lieutenant colonel in the SOAR division. Wouldn't he know if Bjørn disobeyed an order on a mission or not? She took a step back as the heaviness that had left her earlier settled on her shoulders again. Maybe John was wrong. That was a possibility, wasn't it?

"Wouldn't Bjørn have been dishonorably discharged if he did something like that?" Sadie grasped for any thought that might prove solid.

"I guess there was some confusion." Dad leaned against his open door. "Bjørn didn't reenlist when his tour ended a few months later."

"Then John doesn't know for sure what happened?"

"No, but I still don't want you taking the chance." Worry creased the corners of Dad's eyes.

Sadie stared at her dad over the top of the car. He'd always been overprotective of her and Violet, even though he let them go on his adventures with him. She loved that he cherished them, but sometimes his concern felt more stifling than caring. But what if Bjørn had done what John said? Did it matter?

Sadie swallowed the lump in her throat and stepped back. "I'm sorry, Dad. I can't turn down this opportunity." She bent to pick up her keys. "I gotta go."

"Sadie." Dad's exasperation needled her with guilt.

She shut the door with a snap and a wave. Pulling out of the parking lot, she avoided eye contact. She pressed her lips together and rubbed her temple at the headache forming. She couldn't just stop training because Bjørn might have done something wrong in the past, especially since he'd gone out of his way to help them. Her dad had always sworn she could tell the heart of a person by the actions they did, and Bjørn Rebel's actions screamed he was trustworthy.

Chapter Eight

BJØRN WATCHED Sadie across the booth as she dragged her fry through the concoction she'd made out of ketchup and mustard. She waved at a couple as they walked through the door, then pulled her sleeve down over her wrist. Bjørn wrinkled his forehead. Why did she always do that? Why was she in a long-sleeved shirt, for that matter? The summer sun burned hot that afternoon, vanishing all the clouds by noon and making him sweat.

"I still can't believe how well Rowdy did today." She grabbed her glass of iced tea and pointed it at him. "I think you had a big part in that. Bringing that tennis ball was genius. It not only had Rowdy equating you and the chopper with fun, but got him connecting with you."

Bjørn shook his head at the compliment, though he wanted to stand up and cheer that he'd made a good impression. "No, the genius part was how you kept him calm as the rotors fired up. Whatever you've done with him has worked. He only showed a little hesitance."

Bjørn still marveled at the dog's lack of reaction. "After that, he was cool as a cucumber."

"Super Dog." She winked, tossed a half-eaten fry on her plate, and pushed it to the edge of the table. "So, you said you have six siblings, one who is a pararescueman. What do the others do?"

"Well, Lena was an army medic turned bodyguard for a private security firm. Now she's married and helps her husband with his business. Tiikâan has a guide business in the Interior. He's a bush pilot." Bjørn took a drink of his soda. "Magnus is a smokejumper. Sunny takes people to the top of Denali, and Astryd owns a commercial fishing vessel."

With each name, Sadie's jaw dropped lower and lower. Man, she was adorable. She snapped it shut and shrugged.

"So, nothing special." She feigned nonchalance.

"Nah. Just your typical Alaskan family." Bjørn chomped on some ice.

"Are you kidding me?" She laughed, and the sound tumbled down his spine and made him smile. "That's extreme, even for Alaska."

"Normally a family will have one, maybe two rebels. Us, well …" Bjørn's smile stretched across his face at the thought of his family. "Dad always said if we weren't living up to our name, we were doing something wrong."

"Because you wouldn't want the name Rebel and be something like an accountant." Sadie nodded in seriousness. The noise in the restaurant increased as a group of tourists came in, and Bjørn leaned forward to hear her better. "It just wouldn't be right."

"Exactly."

She chuckled as she pulled papers out of her back-pack. "Should we get busy planning our next go with the chopper?"

It was why they had met for dinner. At some point, dinner had turned from a business meeting to a date. At least for him. She obviously had more focus than he did, which was funny since he was the one with the lists.

"Sure. What are you thinking? Are we taking to the air or keeping our heads out of the clouds?" It surprised him he didn't care if they went flying.

He'd had fun that morning, seemed to every time he was around Sadie. The tourists cheered as another group walked in, and the volume of the group increased. If any more showed up, he wouldn't be able to think, let alone hold a conversation.

Sadie shook her head with a smile and said something.

"What?" Bjørn leaned closer, the table pushing into his gut.

"They're a fun bunch," Sadie yelled, her smile getting bigger and her deep brown eyes sparkling with joy.

She seemed to feed off the energy, even if they could barely hear each other. The crowd's arrival gave him an idea, though. He stood, stacked their plates on his corner of the table, then slid into the booth next to her.

"I don't want to have to yell." Bjørn stopped with a hands-width between them.

Sadie went from relaxed to tense in a nanosecond. The maps shook as she set them on the table, and her breaths rasped so loud he could hear her over the crowd. He scooted away, his heart shrinking in his chest.

"I didn't mean to make you uncomfortable." He

went to get out and move back across the booth, but her hand clamped around his forearm stopping him.

"It's ... it's not you." She closed her eyes. Her lips trembled as she licked them. "It's stupid, really." She peeked at him with teary eyes before slamming her lids back closed. "I hate feeling trapped."

Her fingers tightened on his arm, and he slid his fingers over them. He knew all about fears. Wasn't that why he always sat facing the door? That he hadn't thought about that as he'd moved to sit next to her had him hoping he could ease her fear like she'd made him forget about his.

"Would it help if you were on the outside?" He rubbed his fingers along the back of hers. "If not, I can move back to the other side."

"I can—" She swallowed and gazed at him. "You'd switch seats?"

Her fingers unclenched from his arm and threaded through his. With her staring at him with such apprecia-tion, his body coursed with energy, like he'd just chugged four shots of espresso. He'd probably fly the chopper to the moon and back if she asked him to.

"If it helps, absolutely," he said.

He squeezed her fingers, drawing her attention to them. From the furrow in her forehead, she didn't remember almost bruising him. He scooted out of the booth, pulling her with him until she stood next to him. With his free hand, he rubbed the back of his fingers against the still-pale skin of her jaw.

He leaned toward her to be heard over the din of the tourists. "That it means I get to stay close to you, makes it even better."

She let out a shaky breath that blew against his neck.

Her eyes darted back and forth as if she searched for something in his expression. He hoped she found it. He gave her a one-sided smile, let go of her hand, and slid into the booth. Rearranging the maps she'd brought, he watched her out of his peripheral as she stared at her fingers as they clenched and unclenched. She unnerved him, but it looked like the feeling was mutual. Hopefully, she saw it as a positive thing, like he did.

She pulled at her sleeves and slid in next to him. His muscles relaxed into the vinyl seat as his tension leached out of him. He motioned with his hand at the maps.

"Ready for mission planning?" He reached across the table and grabbed his water. "Do you have a COA yet?"

"COA?" She looked at him with a slight smile and one eyebrow raised.

"Course of Action for our MDMP." He pushed his lips together to keep from laughing.

She shook her head as giggles bubbled out. "MDMP?"

He sighed in feigned exasperation. "Military decision-making process, like that wasn't obvious."

"Oh." Her smile widened and her cheeks pinked. "Right. MDMP. I'm guessing it involves lists."

"Very detailed ones." He bumped his shoulder against hers. "Now you're catching on."

She scooted closer, so her heat radiated toward him. Bjørn wanted to pump his hand in success. Playing it cool seemed the better option. He didn't want her jumping away.

"Rowdy did so well today, I think we could try taking off." She leaned her elbow on the table, resting her cheek on her hand as she looked at him. "We'd have to play it by ear, see how he reacted. If he doesn't get overly stressed, we could find a close place to go and play. If he looks like he's not ready, we can touch right back down and do more acclimating at the airport."

"That sounds like a good plan." He nodded and sifted through the maps to find the one he needed. "My brother Gunnar has a house out on the highway. It has a nice open meadow behind it. It'd only be a five-minute flight."

She leaned closer, looking at the location. She then followed the terrain behind Gunnar's and tapped a location on the map. Her shoulder pressed against his, making it hard to think.

"That would be perfect, actually." She grabbed her ponytail that had fallen over her shoulder and pulled on it as she thought. "I could go out there earlier and lay a trail for Rowdy to follow just in case he's adapting to flying fine. If he's not, then I'll just hike out later, maybe take Reggie, my friend's dog I'm training, out by car for a training session."

"I could go with you when you set up the trail, if you want." His pulse roared in his ears, drowning out the restaurant.

Her hand stilled in her ponytail while her leg, a mere inch from his, started bouncing. She didn't need his help with that. Was he coming on too strong? He hadn't been this unsure about what to do since he joined the army. Maybe he should take some time to lay out a MDMP for how to proceed with Sadie.

"I—"

"Glad to know my daughter follows my advice." Will Wilde's stern voice interrupted Sadie.

Her eyes widened, then narrowed as she turned to her dad. "How do you know I'm not?"

Will looked pointedly at Bjørn, then back to his daughter. Bjørn's spine snapped straight as a prickling sensation lifted the hairs on his scalp. Being stuck in the booth suddenly felt like the wrong move to make. He relaxed back against the seat and rested his arm on the table. He could at least pretend his heart wasn't threatening to pound out of his chest.

Why would Will have a problem with him? It wasn't like he and Sadie had done anything wrong. Shoot, from the way Sadie's leg had about bounced a hole in the floor a moment before, she most likely wasn't interested.

"I talked to my cousin in SOAR." Will turned his penetrating gaze to Bjørn, and his hands slicked with sweat.

"Dad." Sadie elongated the vowel in warning.

Will ignored her. "Said there was concern surrounding one of your missions."

That was one way to put it.

"Yeah?" Bjørn had explained the mission so many times, he could rattle it off in his sleep. Didn't mean he owed Will anything, especially if his cousin was just repeating the rumors that had spread like wildfire.

Will's eyes narrowed. "He said your insubordination cost men their lives."

"Hmm." Bjørn ground his teeth as white-hot anger flushed his body. The problem with rumors was that no one cared when the truth came out. People latched on to the first wave of scathing info, only to not care when it was retracted, most likely because there was new and juicier gossip to listen to. If Will's cousin had looked into the official reports before running his mouth, he'd have seen the army had cleared Bjørn of any wrongdoing.

Will shifted on his feet and placed his fists on his hips. "Well?"

Bjørn huffed a short, humorless laugh, shaking his head in disappointment. He had looked forward to helping with SAR, had been dreaming about it almost as long as he had about joining the military. It had always been the plan: get training in the military to be the best pilot he could, then use that training to save lives back home. Looked like that dream was blown from the sky, falling in a fiery ball of dashed hopes to the ground.

Bjørn pulled out his wallet and threw more than enough money on the table to cover dinner. "I should—"

"Dad, back off, okay?" Sadie placed her hand on top of Bjørn's, and he froze.

"John said not to trust him." Will's finger pointed at Bjørn and fired hurt straight to his heart.

"Well, John's wrong." Sadie pushed from the booth and squared off with her dad. "You even said he doesn't have specifics. I'm taking your advice, you know, the one you drilled into us as children?" She poked the big man in the chest. "Judge people by their actions, not by others' opinions. Remember that one? Or does that no longer apply?"

Man, she was a firecracker. Bjørn didn't want to cause this family fight, but her defense of him shifted his resentment to hopefulness. She snagged all her maps from the table and shoved them into her backpack.

"Come on, Bjørn." The fire in her eyes sparked excitement in him. "This place isn't the best for planning." She grabbed his hand and pulled him from the booth. "Too many annoying distractions."

She glared at her dad as she dragged Bjørn toward the door. He should stay and explain to Will what had happened, but if Will believed every rumor that came across his path, then maybe Bjørn didn't want to mess with the drama that created. Besides, the firecracker had her hand clutched in his, shooting sparks up his arm. Hopefully, following her didn't blow up in his face.

Chapter Nine

SADIE STOMPED TO HER CAR, her neck hot with anger at her dad's audacity. She had never, not once growing up, been embarrassed by her parents. Dad's behavior back there had all kinds of emotions jumbling up within her. She stopped next to her car, her gaze lingering on the restaurant, hoping her dad would come out to apologize.

She swallowed as embarrassment won the battle for her attention. A tingle swept up the back of her neck, making her ears hot. She had to fix this.

"I'm so—"

"Don't." Bjørn squeezed her hand, reminding her she still clung to it. "Don't apologize. You did a lot more for me back there than a lot of my so-called friends did."

He rubbed his thumb over the back of her hand as he stared across the street to the bay. It was an absent-minded motion, but it tumbled waves of awareness through her. If she hadn't come to his defense, he would've just left. Did that mean Dad was right?

"Why didn't you defend yourself?" Her question stilled his hand. She worried her tone was still sharp as her anger toward her dad burned off.

Bjørn didn't answer right away, just stared at a fishing boat as it puttered out to sea. When he did, his voice was low and filled with hurt.

"Want to take a walk?" He pointed with his chin to the sidewalk across Railway Avenue that led to Waterfront Park.

"Yeah, just let me toss my pack in my car." She pulled the strap from her shoulder and reluctantly dropped his hand.

He flexed his fingers a few times before shoving both hands into his jean pockets. She pressed her lips tight with disappointment as she tossed her pack in the backseat of her vehicle. Wishing she'd brought a dog so she'd have something to do with her hands, she pushed them into her vest pockets and balled them into fists.

They walked along the sidewalk in silence. He'd nod at people as they passed but seemed drawn into himself. Dang her dad and his jumping to conclusions. She and Bjørn had had such a nice evening talking about nothing in particular. They'd only gotten one training session planned. She had hoped to get several.

She glanced at him out of the corner of her eye, quickly pulling her gaze back to the sidewalk in front of her. Why had he asked to come with her to stage the training field past his brother's place? The warm look he'd given her as he'd asked had sent her stomach into a riot of nerves, like a litter of puppies had suddenly woken up and wanted to play. She wanted to stomp back to the restaurant and growl at her dad some more for interrupting.

She inwardly huffed as she tightened her ponytail. Bjørn's silence unnerved her even more than his gazes had. She tucked her thumbs against the palms of her hands with her fingers as she let her arms swing softly beside her. Could she find enough things for the show if he decided not to help anymore? She wouldn't blame him. She'd definitely have second thoughts if someone started throwing accusations around.

Bjørn stepped closer to her as a family passed, and the back of his hand brushed against hers. She uncurled her hands. She wanted to be bold and slide her fingers into his. The heat of anger that had pushed aside her normal hesitance in the restaurant and had propelled her to grab his hand had burned off to leave embarrassment and shame. Layer that with her usual self-doubt, and she didn't have a hope of digging up the bravery to push past that boundary again.

When the family passed, he didn't move away. She held her breath, keeping her gaze firmly on the sidewalk ahead of them. His hand brushed hers again, and she let her breath out in a slow, shaky stream. He cleared his throat. Her own suddenly felt dry, like it was closing up on her.

"Let's go sit." He snagged her index finger with his and pulled her toward a bench down on the rocky beach.

When he had her going where he wanted, and she thought he'd drop her hand, he threaded his fingers through her own. Her entire body lit with joy. She now understood why her dogs' bodies would wag from head to tail when they got really excited. Her normal energy multiplied exponentially, and she wanted to dance a jig.

She stifled the desire … barely.

They sat on the bench, the wake from a passing boat making the water slap against the rocky shore. He set their joined hands on his thigh, then absentmindedly rubbed the back of hers with his other. Her pulse increased like the boat motor opening up as it headed to sea. Would he notice her scars barely hidden by her cuff? She pulled on the front of her vest and shirt, sweating in the hot summer evening. Of course, the weather had to choose that day to be beautiful. She should've left her vest in her car.

She tried to relax, to let the lazy circles he drew on her skin ease her tense muscles. She closed her eyes and focused on the slow motion. The more she concentrated on his rough skin skimming over hers, the more tingling built from her hand, spreading up her arm. Her skin was on fire again, but this time, the unnerving burn felt glorious. She shifted on the bench, wanting him to stop before he found her scars, but needing the touch more than she ever thought possible.

"About two months before my discharge, I had a mission taking a special ops team into a hot zone." His soft words pulled her attention from the confusing sensation on her arm.

His cheek muscle clenched, and his Adam's apple bobbed. He sighed, and the hand threaded with hers squeezed. Her eyes widened as realization dawned.

He didn't like talking about what happened.

Or was it he just didn't want to tell her? She should stop him before he started, let him know she didn't care what happened, but her father's behavior kept her mouth shut. Maybe if she knew what had gone wrong, she could get her father to see reason. She squeezed his hand in encouragement.

"I can't tell you specifics." He blew out a short, humorless laugh. "Telling you anything at all could get me in trouble, but I want you—that is, I'd like for your opinion of me to be based on what actually happened."

"I don't care what happened." She turned on the bench so she angled toward him. "You've shown who you are in your actions." She thought about how much the dogs loved him, and a small smile pushed her lips up. "Besides, my dogs adore you. They're a much better judge of character than anyone I know."

He stared at her, his serious expression pushing her joking away. Heat spread from her chest to her arms, making it hard to breathe. Or maybe that was because of the intensity of his gaze glued to hers. A cool breeze blew salty air over her, pulling strands from her ponytail.

He lifted his hand from where it had stilled its circling pattern on her skin and tucked the strand behind her ear. He trailed his fingers along her jawline before returning his hand to its motion on the back of her hand. Never had she been more thankful for a bench than at that moment. Her muscles trembled at his touch, and her knees surely would've buckled.

"Thank you for trusting me." He shook his head slightly. "You don't know how much that means to me." He looked at their joined hands and continued. "The mission was a recon only of the enemy's camp to see if the rumors of weapons were true. Situated in a series of canyons and mountains made getting a signal back to base nearly impossible and, because of the sensitive nature of the mission, the CO ordered radio silence between us and base. The terrain also made infiltration tricky, especially at night." He sighed. "I was to land four clicks out and wait for the team's return. The mission was only supposed to take an hour and a half max, and it would've if the team leader, a guy known for taking risky chances and his jerky tendencies, hadn't gone all Rambo on us."

He clenched his jaw again, pain and anger in his voice, and turned his face away from her. He watched another boat trolling by. She wanted to wrap her free hand around his arm and lean into him. Instead, she tucked her foot under her knee and picked at the bottom of her jeans.

"About forty-five minutes after the team left, the radio started exploding with shouts. The team leader had slipped into the camp to 'get a closer look.'" He used air quotes and huffed. "He did nothing but get caught, bringing an angry ants' nest down on the team. I radioed to them an alternative extraction point, but he shot me down. Commanded me to stay where I was." His voice got tight with emotion. "Do you know how hard it was to sit there and listen to the team, my friends, yelling about another man down?"

Tears pricked her eyes, and she wrapped her hand around his arm and scooted closer.

"After fifteen minutes of it, I radioed in a closer rendezvous and went and got them. When we arrived back at the base and debriefed, Rambo concocted a story about it being my fault since I disobeyed his orders and didn't come get them earlier."

"No!" she gasped, snapping up and looking at him. "And the commander believed him?"

"With base issuing radio silence between us and them, there wasn't any way to prove him wrong." Bjørn settled back into the bench. "A few of the guy's team disputed the accusation, but it still took time to sort out.

Somehow, he was even able to get the mission recording from our communications deleted. It wasn't until his team went out on another mission and he botched that one, too, that the rest of his team came forward about what really happened. But it was too late to clean up all the rumors that had circulated, still are circulating from what your dad said."

"I'm so sorry," she whispered past the pain in her throat.

No wonder he hadn't wanted to defend himself. He'd spent more than enough time doing that before. He shouldn't have it follow him here.

"I did mess up, so I deserve the criticism." His hand loosened in hers, but she didn't let go. "I should have gone in when things first blew up. I had the alternative extraction point set up. If I would have just went with my gut, we may not have lost the soldiers we did on that mission."

"That wasn't your fault." She squeezed his arm in a hug. "He shouldn't have done what he did to begin with. If he would've stuck to the plan, all the team would've made it back, probably without the camp ever knowing."

"Yeah, you're right. It's just …" His voice trailed off, and she wondered if he would continue.

Though it went against every atom in her body, she stayed silent. She mirrored his slow, steady breathing against her arm. Longing for him to continue warred with worry for what he would say. He took a deep breath, and she tipped her head to watch him.

"It's just that my failure to get to them in time and their deaths hang on me like a cloak of shadows I can't take off." Bjørn's next breath shuddered in and out. "All those I lost over the years shroud over me. Their memories hurt, but comfort at the same time, egg me to do better, to stretch myself further to save more lives." He shook his head with a self-deprecating laugh. "Why am I telling you this?"

"I'm glad you did." She hugged his arm tightly, clamping his hand between hers.

He finally glanced down at her, his intense gaze pooling her insides into molten lava. "Me too."

She leaned her head on his shoulder and let out an inaudible sigh. This man was unlike any she'd ever known. He'd experienced more than she'd ever imagined and had the weight of those echoes on him like scars. Here was a man who might see her own disfigurement and not turn away in disgust.

Chapter Ten

BJØRN WENT through his pre-flight checklist for the third time. Will's accusations from the night before still had Bjørn on edge, wanting to make sure everything checked off perfectly, so there'd be no mistakes. His tour should arrive within the next ten minutes. Even though it was a simple flight to the glacier for a picnic and back, his nerves still frayed a bit on the edges.

He tossed the clipboard onto the pilot's seat and huffed. Pushing his hand through his hair, he stared out at the calm water of Resurrection Bay, trying to suppress his disappointment. How could that mission that had ended his military career with an ashy taste in his mouth have followed him home? What if Will started spreading word about Bjørn not being trustworthy? He'd have to pull up roots and move again.

He kicked a rock into the grass. He liked it there. Liked the small-town community and how the mountains towered right out of the sea. More than anything, he enjoyed being around Sadie and her abundance of energy and drive.

He closed his eyes and thought of the feel of her soft skin beneath his fingertips as he'd rubbed lazy circles across her hand. Her look of adoration as he'd poured out his soul had eased his muscles, bound tight with stress. He still couldn't believe he'd told her all that. He'd only ever told the military counselor.

They'd stayed on that bench, sitting in silence for at least half an hour. Her head resting on his shoulder and her warmth against his side had pushed the bitter memories aside. The feeling had lingered after walking back hand in hand and long into the night. The thought of her quiet acceptance and instant defense even made falling asleep easier, like she stood at the door to his mind, guarding against memories that liked to twist and torment his dreams.

Bjørn had to fix Will's opinion of him. He didn't want to come between Sadie and Will, but he also wasn't willing to leave what was building between him and Sadie. He hated defending himself, but he'd tell Will what happened if it would help. Hopefully, Will would see reason. But Bjørn knew that once a reputation was earned, it was hard to shed it.

His phone rang in his pocket. He pulled it out, his eyebrows winging up in surprise at seeing Will's name on the screen. His hands slicked with sweat, and he hated that this situation made him this nervous.

"Hello?" He walked around his chopper to ease his tension.

"Bjørn? Will, here." Will's words clipped out fast and short. "A plane spotted a boat wreck. The pilot circled the island but couldn't see any survivors. It's in a tricky spot, shallow waters and lots of reef to get caught on. Think you can fly a team in?"

Bjørn's knee-jerk reaction was to say no, especially without any kind of apology from Will for the night before. However, people could be dying. Bjørn couldn't not go, even if he had a problem with Will.

"I have to make a few phone calls, rearrange a tour, but, yeah, I'll be ready when your team gets here." Bjørn grabbed the clipboard from his seat and flipped to the client's information.

Will grunted. "Appreciate it. The team is on the way."

"Okay."

"Keep in contact." Will clipped out the reply.

"Yep." With Bjørn's answer, Will hung up.

Bjørn didn't know what to think. Was Will's declaration to Sadie that Bjørn couldn't be trusted just regarding her, or did Will just have no other options for this rescue mission? Bjørn shook off his confusion and pulled up his buddy's number. Hopefully, he wasn't busy today and could take his tour.

Bjørn was just ending the call with his clients, explaining the situation and the need to change to a new pilot, when Sadie pulled up with Violet and Kemp. He waved, his heart doing a ridiculous dance in his chest at the sight of Sadie smiling through the windshield at him.

Drew's SUV pulled in behind Sadie with Bo, the cameraman. They were taking a chance with taping this rescue mission? Bjørn marched up to Sadie's vehicle as she clipped a leash to Rowdy's collar and let him out.

His mind raced with the anxiety that often happened before an intense mission. He acknowledged its presence, then pushed it aside, letting it simmer in the back of his brain. From his years of experience, he knew he couldn't smother it completely. In fact, the constant burn of it kept him sharp and focused on what needed done.

"Drew's coming?" Bjørn nodded at Drew over the top of her car.

"Yeah." Sadie pulled on her sleeves as her gaze darted to Drew and back. "He was at the kennel when we got the call and thought a rescue would be perfect for the show. It was already part of the contract, with us training SAR dogs and all, though we made sure the people we rescue will be given the chance to decline their segment being aired. Plus, Drew and the cameramen should be good at noticing things, so I figured the extra help couldn't hurt."

"That's true." Bjørn bent and rubbed Rowdy's ears, keeping his voice cheerful. "Think Rowdy is ready for this? We haven't done the training we talked about."

"I don't know." Sadie bit her lip and frowned. "He did well the other day and seems excited to be here. He's great with rescues, really catches things all of us miss, so I hate to not take him." Her forehead wrinkled, and she ran her hand over her face. "Maybe it's better to leave him in the car and have Aurora or Denali come get him."

Bjørn hated that he'd made her doubt. That hadn't been his intention. It was just not the way they had planned. Would he always stick with his stupid lists? He wanted to be more like Sadie, grabbing opportunities as they came. Not always writing out the pros and cons with a detailed action plan. He slid his hand along her shoulders, relishing how her muscles relaxed at his touch.

"I'm sure it'll be fine." Bjørn pulled her in a sideways hug before letting go. "Rowdy is amazing, and he'll do just about anything for you." The dog wasn't the only one. "Even if the flight stresses him out a little, I'm sure once we touch down, you'll get him calmed down."

"You're right." Sadie nodded with determination. "You ready for us to load up?"

"Yep." Bjørn walked backward toward the chopper. "Welcome to Rebel Air, your adventure in the Alaskan skies."

Violet chuckled as she stepped up next to Sadie. Sadie glanced at Violet and shook her head, rolling her eyes. He remembered how, in the military, joking with whatever special ops unit he was transporting helped ease the stress of the coming mission and relax the nerves a little, so he leaned on that experience, hoping it worked in the SAR missions too.

"The copilot seat is reserved for the smartest in the bunch." He pointed at Drew who held a small camera pointing at Bjørn. "Drew, that means you're out."

"Oh, burn." Violet clapped and skipped toward the chopper, shooting finger guns at Drew.

Drew turned the camera around. "A man can't get any love around here."

Violet climbed into the door, crouched down, and motioned everyone close. "Gather up, everyone. Let's have a quick prayer, then get in the air." She smiled a one-sided grin. "Since I'm obviously the smartest, evidence that wonderful poem, I ride shotgun."

Violet bowed her head. Bjørn followed suit, only to jump when Sadie's hand slid into his. He squeezed it when she went to pull away and wrapped his other around it, so hers was sandwiched in between his. Violet's impassioned prayer for the lives of those lost and that the SAR team would have eyes to see them settled the last of Bjørn's doubts. No matter what Will believed, Bjørn would help, as long as he could.

Chapter Eleven

THE FOLLOWING DAY, Sadie tipped the last puppy upside down for the Super Dog training, then placed her on the damp towel. With her mind off in la-la land, she had needed more focus than necessary to get her to-do list done. Well, her version of a list. The scrawling on the back of her hand probably couldn't compare to whatever Bjørn had for his day.

And there her mind went again.

She hadn't been able to think about much else after the rescue the day before. It wasn't just the way being around him made her heart race, either. His focus while on the mission amazed her. Just by studying the wreckage as they hovered above it and, from the evidence he saw, he'd zeroed in on where survivors would have most likely gone. He must've learned that in the military, like a form of reconnaissance or something. He'd landed in a tiny clearing on an island, barely big enough for the rotors to squeeze in, and within thirty minutes, Rowdy had scented the survivors.

Sadie also couldn't keep the excitement of how well

Rowdy had done contained. He hadn't balked once on the helicopter ride. The minute they touched down and she gave the command to search, he was all business. She learned so much from the dog, some days she wondered if he wasn't the one actually training her.

Pulling out a pen from her pocket, she crossed off Super Dog on her hand. She read the next thing on the list and groaned. She hated cleaning out the fridge. They all took turns with the chores, and this month she got fridge duty. The others had left notes, more like threats, that if it didn't get done, she'd get all the cleaning duties. She marched toward the front of the kennel. She'd put it off as long as she could.

The door opened, and the bell howled to announce the visitor. She smiled as Scott, the delivery person for The Rez, stepped in with a coffee and paper bag. Jealousy for whoever had ordered reared its ugly head and made her stomach growl in complaint. Maybe she should follow Scott back to work and grab her own coffee and snack.

"Just the person I'm looking for." He extended the items to her.

Her head shook as she snatched them from him like a ravenous wolverine. "I didn't order."

"Someone ordered for you." He pointed to the bag. "There's a note in there with the scone."

Scott's laugh followed him out the door as she tore into the bag. The lemony scent crashed over her, and she closed her eyes and inhaled. She pulled the note out. For once something other than the pastry drew her focus.

Sadie,

I'm lost and need your help. I think it might be because you've addled my brain and make it hard to think straight. Bring your search team, but leave the cameras behind. I bought myself a lemon scone for the trail, just in case Rowdy and Reggie can't find me.

Bjørn

Sadie laughed as her pulse sped up like rotor blades on a helicopter. The *ch-ch* of her blood rushing through her veins pounded in her ears. Was he planning on leaving crumbs like Hansel and Gretel? Or was he implying she could sniff out a scone better than the dogs? She shrugged as she broke off a piece of pastry and popped it into her mouth. He was probably right. She rushed into the supply room, grabbed her gear, then poked her head into Aurora's office.

"Bjørn's hiding in the woods. The dogs and I are supposed to go find him." Sadie couldn't help the joy in her voice, her list completely forgotten.

"He's hiding? Like hide and seek?" Aurora's head snapped up, and she pushed her glasses back in place.

Sadie snorted at the thought of Bjørn huddling in a hiding place. "Yeah. Exactly like that." She waved and jogged to get the dogs.

Twenty minutes later, her head buzzing with Mexican mocha and her excitement building to new levels, she pulled in next to Bjørn's truck in what she assumed was his brother's place. Sled dogs yipped from the dog yard, announcing her arrival. She got Rowdy and Reggie out, had them sniff the bag with the lemon scone and Bjørn's vehicle, and unhooked the leashes.

"Go find Bjørn." Sadie motioned her arm toward the woods, and both dogs' noses hit the ground.

They circled the truck, then zigged and zagged through the meadow grass. She followed behind them, taking in the fireweed still only blossoming near the bottom of the stalk. She loved how the flower showed the length of summer with its pretty, purply pink. Though, when the color only graced the top in a few months, part of her would wish summer could hold out a little longer.

Rowdy barked one sharp yip, then shot straight through the grass. He'd caught the scent, his short tail wagging like crazy. Reggie fell in next to Rowdy and bayed in success. Sadie jogged behind them, keeping the dogs in sight. She didn't have to worry about Rowdy. He never went farther than he could see her. Reggie, on the other hand, sometimes wandered.

With each step, her heart thrashed faster and faster in her chest like a school of fish caught in a bubble net. Her lungs squeezed tight, and at any minute, nerves would consume her ... or was it hope? Ugh, she couldn't think straight.

She paused and took as deep a breath as she could. The warm summer air, full of fresh pine, clean meadow grass, and damp dirt, cleared her jumbled thoughts. A mosquito buzzed in her ear. She swatted it and jogged after the dogs.

She could speculate all day, worry she was setting herself up for heartache, but the reality was, Bjørn had already snagged her with his kindness and unselfish pursuits. What she should do was swim hard and fast in the opposite direction to snap the line tugging her to him. She wasn't even struggling, not one bit, as he reeled her in. Shoot, she was probably one of those fish that swallowed the whole dang hook.

The dogs veered off toward the glacier, and Sadie rushed to catch up. The glacial till fields were always a pain to traverse with the patches of melting ice, dirt, and rocks all jumbled together. Reggie's shorter beagle legs might not make it.

She climbed over a large deposit to find Rowdy pointing at the wall of ice. No. She shook her head in denial. Bjørn hadn't actually gone into the glacier, had he? Terror crashed over her, and her chest squeezed for a completely different reason than a moment before.

"Rowdy, Reggie, wait! Stop!"

She couldn't … she couldn't actually go in there. She stepped up to the fissure in the ice, her legs stiff like wood. The blue tint of snow, ice, and sun narrowed and disappeared as the opening twisted to the right. The memory of the avalanche crashing into her, pushing her against the hot stove, then trapping her in frigid cement assaulted her, making her legs and arms shake with the need to run far away.

What if this was an actual rescue, and people were lost? She closed her eyes, gritting her teeth against the tears stinging to be let loose. This was supposed to be a training session for the dogs, not for her. She was Rowdy's handler. If she couldn't go into the situations where people needed help, she was wasting her, the dogs', and her family's time and money.

The image of her best friend, Melinda, frozen in the avalanche, assaulted Sadie's mind and made her shudder. She couldn't allow her fear to let someone else die. Rowdy whined at her feet and licked her fingers. She balled her clammy hands and stared down the opening.

What would she do if one of her dogs balked? She'd ease them into it, that's what she'd do. Huffing out a sharp breath, she swallowed. Well, she'd just have to ease herself into it too.

She motioned for the dogs to search. "Go. Go find Bjørn." Her voice came out tight.

The dogs yipped and took off into the crevasse. Taking a deep breath, like it would be her last, she followed after them. Her feet slipped on the slick ice. Each step farther into the cold coffin twisted her stomach into a tighter knot.

The dogs' barks echoed around her, confusing her as the trail turned deeper into the ice. How far had she gone? Twenty feet? A hundred? The farther she went, the colder it grew. She pulled the sleeves of her sweatshirt over her hands.

A thunderous pop boomed around her, and she froze. Was the glacier shifting? She frantically darted her gaze above her and to each side, her breathing becoming more and more rapid. She didn't want to be trapped again. Didn't want to die encased in ice and snow like Melinda.

"Rowdy." Her voice, barely a whisper, cracked. "Bjørn. Help."

Her legs shook so violently they wouldn't hold her. She crouched to the ground, tucking her face between her knees. Her pulse roared in her ears, like the roaring of the avalanche had filled her with terror all those years before. She was there again, tumbling and twisting in frigid cold and burning metal. A scream filled the space, and she didn't know if it was Melinda's or her own. The ice pressed down on her like concrete blocks, and she couldn't breathe.

Chapter Twelve

AT THE SIGHT of Sadie and the dogs crossing the glacial till, Bjørn tucked into the gap he'd found in the glacier's wall. Good. She'd come by herself. Excitement rushed through his body like jet fuel igniting as the beautiful blue ice surrounded him.

He didn't go far, maybe just a hundred yards in. He hadn't really made a plan beyond giving something for the dogs to hunt up and, hopefully, getting Sadie alone without the camera crew. Which was so unlike him, he wasn't sure if he should celebrate the deviation or go get checked out at the clinic. Originally, he planned on just finding a copse of trees or a jumble of rocks to wait by, but when he'd spied the glacier, he hoped it would give the dogs a challenge.

The sound of Reggie baying bounced loud off of the ice walls and echoed around Bjørn. So much for his hiding being a challenge. Would the dogs run right in? He stopped at a spot that widened and turned to face the way he'd come. Eagerness to see Sadie's reaction charged him, making his insides quiver with nerves and a silly smile to stretch across his face.

He scanned the ice walls and marveled at the way the sun filtered through the glacier. Various colors of turquoise, dark blue, and white filled the space. It was almost like he was underwater, but backward with the way the ice formed peaks like small waves above and around him. Some might even say the small cave was romantic. He certainly couldn't wait to show Sadie what he'd found and explore a little deeper in together.

Reggie's baying picked back up, and Bjørn bounced on his toes in anticipation. Less than thirty seconds later, Rowdy's smiling face bolted from around the corner. His tongue hung from his mouth, and his short, brown tail wagged like crazy. Reggie quickly followed him, letting out a loud bay that made Bjørn tuck one ear against his shoulder.

"Good boys. You found me." Bjørn bent down and rubbed each dog's ears.

Grabbing the dog treats from his pocket, he had them sit before handing them the reward. He peered toward the opening. Why was it taking Sadie so long to get there?

Rowdy's entire body froze, his head cocking back the way he'd come. All at once, the hair rose on Bjørn's scalp, sending a sinking feeling to his gut. Rowdy took off for the entrance, and Bjørn raced after the dog.

A scream full of agony ricocheted off the walls, sending a fresh wave of goosebumps across his skin. He shouldn't have come into this cave. He should've stayed where he could monitor their approach. Predators riddled this area. Shoot, he'd left a trail of crumbs leading right to her.

He'd almost reached the entrance, each step pummeling his brain with what danger had befallen Sadie, when he turned a corner to find her huddled over her feet. Her hands wrapped tightly around her head, and she rocked back and forth. Crap. He'd forgotten about her fear of being trapped. He rushed to her side.

"Bjørn, help." Her terrified voice pricked his eyes with tears.

"Sadie, I'm here. It's okay." He bent down beside her, but it was like she didn't hear him. He rubbed his hand down her back. "Let's get out of here."

She curled further in on herself, a tremble shaking her entire body. "Help."

"Hey. I've got you." He wrapped her in his arms and lifted her up. "I've got you."

Her sobs broke his heart as she buried her face in his neck. Her hand clung to his sweatshirt, pulling the fabric tight against his body. How could he have possibly forgotten something so important? This is what happened when he didn't follow his plans.

"I'm so sorry, Sadie." He choked out the apology through a tight throat.

Emerging into the warm sun, he rushed to a boulder close to the entrance and sat. She clawed up his body like she tried to get to safety. He did this to her. His hand trembled as he pushed her hair that had fallen from her ponytail away from her face.

"Sadie, it's okay." He cupped his hands on her cheeks, and she stilled. "Hey, babe, it's okay. We're out. You're not trapped."

Her eyes widened and darted around, as if just realizing she was in the open. Her hands flexed and opened where they pressed flat against his collarbones. She shuddered and buried her face back in his neck, her body heaving in silent sobs.

Wrapping his arms around her, his own tears threatened to fall. He'd been so focused on impressing her with a difficult situation for the dogs' training that he hadn't even taken her into consideration. He'd just thrown any trust she had in him out the side door of the chopper at thirty-thousand feet.

"I'm so, so sorry." His voice came out ragged with emotion, and he leaned his face against her hair.

She took a deep breath, her head moving from side to side. "Not ... your ... fault."

"I'm such a bonehead." He loosened his arms from around her. The guilt made him want to throw up. "I should've thought about you not wanting to be boxed in."

"No." She sat up, her reddened eyes darting everywhere but his face.

He'd really messed things up. He let his hands fall to rest on the boulder. What he wanted to do was hold her, wipe away her tears still tracking over her freckles, but he'd lost the chance to do that. She'd realize it as soon as the terror completely left.

"This isn't your fault." She ran a finger over the tear-soaked spot on his sweatshirt, her touch making his skin beneath the fabric tingle. She took a shuddering breath, and he wanted to capture her hand in his and comfort her. "When I was eleven years old, I went on a winter camping trip with my dad, my best friend Melinda, and her dad. We got dropped off in this basin where a national park cabin is. Our dads went for a hike to check out an area up the mountain, but Melinda and I stayed behind." Her face wavered in a sad smile. "We were having a card game competition and didn't want to stop."

She swallowed, and the action looked so painful it made Bjørn's throat hurt. She didn't need to tell him all this. He wanted to stop her from living through whatever horror she was about to reveal, but he also knew that telling others, no matter how painful, could be healing. So he kept his lips firmly pressed together and his hands clenched against the boulder.

"It was a warm spring day, and about thirty minutes after they left, a rumbling started shaking the cabin." Her voice hitched. "The avalanche smashed into the cabin, pushing the walls against each other in a jumbled mess. I tumbled in snow and logs until it stopped. The cabin walls had created this pocket of space within the snow, with me cemented in cold on one side and Melinda on the other. It covered her almost all the way up. She couldn't breathe. I kept telling her it'd be all right. I lied." Her face scrunched as fresh tears pooled in her big brown eyes. "She didn't make it."

"Oh, Sadie, I'm so sorry." Bjørn reached up and rubbed her tears away with the back of his fingers, not able to keep from comforting her any longer.

Her next words tumbled out fast, like she just wanted to get the story out and done. "The search crew didn't find us for two hours. The only thing that kept me from losing my feet to frostbite or freezing to death was that I had my boots on to go get more firewood and a sleeping bag ended up within my reach." She finally looked Bjørn in the eyes. "My dad kept saying if they'd had trained search dogs, they could've found us earlier. Maybe Melinda wouldn't have died. Since then, I swore I'd do everything I could to save more people." She fisted his shirt in her hands with a moan. "How can I do that if I can't go where the dogs go? What if someone's trapped and I panic?"

Bjørn cupped the back of her head in his hands and leaned his forehead on hers. He understood the need to help. Wasn't that what drove him? But for her to live through what she did—to not only have to watch her best friend die, but to be trapped with her—would leave a wound hard to heal from. She hadn't run away from the pain. No, she had leaned into it, building her kennel to be a resource that could save others. Bjørn hoped he hadn't messed it up with her permanently because she had captured his heart completely.

"I think, when the moment came and someone was in trouble, you'd push through the fear." His words had her shaking her head, so he pulled back a few inches to look in her eyes. "You care more about others than you do yourself, Sadie, and I know you'd find the strength within to push through, but, if it would help, maybe we could work on your fear a little bit at a time so you can train yourself to focus through it. My military counselor said it's like training your muscles: the more often you do it, the stronger your good responses will get."

"Like I would the dogs in the same situation." Her quiet voice barely lifted above the breeze blowing past them. "You'd do that? You'd help me?"

"I don't think there's anything I wouldn't do for you."

She pressed her palms against his chest and leaned into him. The sweet smell of lemon scone faintly clung to her as she drew near. He froze, unable to think of anything but her approach.

Her tentative touch trembled on his lips. Electrical

synapses fired in his brain, like they'd been dormant until her kiss. The thought lifted him, soaring him into the clouds, as he placed his hands on her cheeks and captured her lips with his. She sighed and wrapped her arms around the back of his neck. This … this was it, the next box to check off on his life's list. In Sadie Wilde's arms and heart was where he wanted to spend the rest of his days.

Chapter Thirteen

SADIE'S SMILE hurt her cheeks as she followed Bjørn's truck to his home. The silly thing hadn't left her face since he'd kissed her senseless by the glacier. She pulled her sweatshirt away from her body to fan herself. That man sure knew how to kiss a woman.

Rowdy whined in the passenger seat and cocked his head at her like she was strange. Her cheeks heated as she glanced at the dog. His eyebrow lifted in a what-are-you-doing expression.

"What?" She cranked on the AC. "He's not like Leo." She stared through the windshield at Bjørn's tailgate, trying to suppress her smile and failing. "He's not like anyone I've ever met."

Though embarrassment still hummed at the bottom of her gut, the possibility of something more, something that felt an awful lot like love, gonged loud in her heart and ears, almost drowning out the shame that always came when she freaked out. She huffed out a breath as her body roasted. When had the day gotten so warm? She pushed up the sleeves of her sweatshirt, revealing her mutilated skin. Her giddiness evaporated like morning fog.

She might have felt brave enough to tell him about the avalanche and Melinda. Or had it been desperation? Whatever emotion propelled her to tell him hadn't been compelling enough to show him the ugliness that catastrophe had left behind. She didn't need the reminders that wrinkled her arms and shoulder like a topographical map to remember the pain and heartache that day held. She heard the avalanche's roar as it rushed to devour her and Melinda almost every night in her dreams. Wasn't that enough?

She yanked the sleeves down, covering half her hands. Something Bjørn had said by the glacier filtered through her agitation. If he thought she could work through her fear of tight spaces, could his counselor's advice help with her stomach dropping every time she looked at her scarred skin? Only one way to find out.

She swallowed down the lump of dread that balled in her throat, then swallowed again when the first time didn't help. With jerky motions, she pushed her sleeves above her elbows. The cool air felt glorious against her skin. She stared through the windshield, trying to keep her eyes on the road and not glued to the nasty ripples on her arms. Rowdy whined and placed his head on the console.

"Maybe." Her voice cracked, and she cleared her throat. "Maybe I should talk to someone, like a counselor or something, about what happened."

Rowdy inched closer, his tail thumping slow like he wasn't sure how to help her. Reggie added his thoughts with a whine from his crate in the back.

"Though my parents took me to a counselor, I never

wanted to talk about what had happened, not really," she said, remembering all the things she'd longed to say to the counselor but couldn't get past her lips.

Rowdy's wet tongue licked her elbow, causing her to flinch.

"You don't mind my scars, do you?" She glanced at the cute dog before returning her attention to the road.

His tail wagged at light speed. It surprised her he wasn't shaking the entire car. She placed her hand on his head and rubbed his ears.

"Maybe if I would've actually talked to the psychologist Mom and Dad took me to, instead of just pretending everything was okay, I wouldn't have this crippling fear or worry so much about what others think of my scars." She sighed. "Or hate them so much myself."

Bjørn pulled into a drive off of Heather Lane, just a short walk from where she lived with Denali and her eleven-year-old son, Sawyer. How were they practically neighbors, and she hadn't known? Large raspberry bushes and tall, white spruce surrounded an older cabin decorated with worn-out buoys and fishing gear. The bright, kelly green trim on the windows and front door gave the worn logs a bit of cheeriness.

Bjørn got out of his truck and waved at her as she pulled to a stop behind him. His dimple creased his cheek and flipped her heart. He was heart-achingly gorgeous. No way someone like him would really want her once he saw her scars, would he?

Yanking down her sleeves, she told her inner doubt to shut up. It was probably stupid not to listen. Her heart would most likely end up ripped from her chest and torn to shreds, but, with the memory of his words, for the first time, maybe ever, she finally felt cherished by someone other than her family. She'd find out eventually if her scars repulsed him like they had the few others she'd dated. Until then, she wanted to let her feelings soar. She pushed open her door and stepped out, bracing herself against the warm metal.

Bjørn jogged up and kissed her on the cheek as he headed to the back of her Land Cruiser. "I'll get Reggie out."

Rowdy tumbled out of the passenger seat and dashed after Bjørn, completely ignoring her. Bjørn rubbed the side of Rowdy's head while he opened the back, where Reggie barked excitedly. Even the dogs loved him. She snatched her backpack from the vehicle and shut the door.

Her heart pounded in her chest, and she wasn't sure if it was excitement or anxiety. She turned away from him and scanned the yard to get her body back to normal. She didn't want to make a fool of herself. Again.

Being outgoing, the one blazing the way in life, especially their business, she was used to shaking off any embarrassment that was bound to happen. She desperately wanted this date, or whatever it was, to happen without another mishap. Breaking down into a quivering mess was enough humiliation for one day.

"The place is still kind of a disaster from the last owner." Bjørn stepped up beside her and threaded his fingers through hers.

Her palm tingled and fingers sizzled like someone had zapped her wrist with a training collar.

"He thought old junk from his fishing boat was decoration." Bjørn scratched his cheek with the opposite hand. "Though, now that I think about it, since he left it all behind, he probably was just lazy."

"It looks like a lot of places here." Living in a fishing community meant boating paraphernalia often became engrained in all of life. "I love how your property backs right up to the mountains. It'd be nice to not have any neighbors behind you. I live with Denali just down the street a bit, but we don't have this sense of seclusion you have here, even though you're in town."

"That's why I bought it. That and the guest cabin out back." He pointed to a quaint cabin she hadn't noticed at the end of the driveway. "The plan is eventually to offer housing along with the chopper tours, but I haven't gotten that crossed off the list yet."

She shook her head and smiled up at him. "You and your lists."

"Don't knock them. They work. Keep me focused." Bjørn stared down at her.

His gaze travelled across her face, like he was memorizing every detail. The attention raised her body temperature even more, making her break out into a sweat. Great. Now she'd stink on top of everything else. His perusal landed on her lips and didn't move.

"What's next on your list?" Her mouth dried out like the Sahara, and her voice came out a throaty whisper.

His mouth lifted on one side in a dangerous smile that threatened to buckle her knees. "You." His declaration had her eyebrows winging to her hairline. He chuckled. "Just hanging out with you, doing whatever you want to do."

Her eyes darted to his lips, like they were a compass and his mouth was north. His smile broadened even wider. She was on hazardous terrain with him, ground she'd never been on before.

"Come on. I'll make us some lunch while you pick a movie to watch." Bjørn pulled her toward the porch. "I don't know about you, but I could use some downtime after this morning."

"Yeah." She whistled to the dogs as he led her up the porch stairs.

Actually, relaxing in front of the TV sounded wonderful. She wasn't much for watching a lot of movies. Dad always said the screen rotted a person's brain, plus there were too many things to get done to just do nothing but sit. Yet, taking a few hours to recuperate from her episode might be the perfect thing to do, especially if it meant she could snuggle up against Bjørn on the couch.

She stepped into his cabin and froze. The inside proved a complete opposite of the outside. Organization reigned in the small, open space. A leather couch sat against four enormous windows that lined the front, looking out at the porch. A dark, stone hearth covered the walls behind a Blaze King wood stove, protecting the walls from the heat. He had perfectly piled a neat stack of firewood on an iron stand next to the stove.

On the opposite side of the room, a rustic kitchen spread along the back corner like an L. Two-by-one board shelves full of spices, coffee, sugar, and other miscellaneous cooking supplies hung above the propane stove. Cast-iron skillets in various sizes dangled from the log beam above the kitchen. One cupboard supported the sink and tiny countertop situated under a window. The frame-structured walls weren't even sheetrocked, just pink insulation shoved between lumber and covered in plastic. So typical of Alaskan homes, the lack of finished walls and plywood flooring didn't surprise her.

What had her gaping like a salmon on the river bank was how meticulous everything was. His desk, placed in the corner by the couch, didn't have a loose paper in sight, just a notebook propped open with a pen in the binding crease. No dishes waited to be washed in the sink. No boxes of cereal hung out on the table. Did everything Bjørn do have to be in order? What would he do if she rearranged his spice shelf?

She pressed her lips together to keep her laugh in and peeked at Bjørn. He ran his hand across the back of his neck, his gaze darting around the room like he was embarrassed. She bit her lip to keep from saying anything.

"I know it's a mess. Just haven't had time to work on it. I'm hoping once winter comes, I can get the sheetrock up and finish the flooring." Bjørn sounded dejected, and Sadie couldn't hold her laugh back.

"Are you kidding me?" She stepped away from him and fingered the books lined on a bookshelf next to his desk. They were in alphabetical order by author. "Do you take hours cleaning and organizing?" She turned back to him and lifted her eyebrow in mirth. "Do you have a list to make sure you don't forget anything?"

He shook his head and waved his finger at her. "Laugh all you want. I've always liked things in their place." He shrugged. "The military kind of multiplied that trait to borderline obsessive heights. Pick out a movie, make yourself comfortable, and I'll warm up some leftovers."

She wandered to the shelf of movies and chuckled at the selection. He had everything from Disney movies to action to even a few romances. What should she pick? If she picked a romance, would he think she was hinting too hard? She had little desire to watch a cartoon, and after her terror-filled adrenaline spike earlier, action held no interest either. She pulled out *The Princess Bride*, deciding it was enough of a mix of everything that hopefully it would do.

"How about a classic?" She held up the movie.

"As you wish." His cheeky smile made her stomach flutter.

After getting the movie cued up on the TV, she turned to the small kitchen. "Need any help?"

"Nope." He pulled a container out of the microwave, filling the room with the savory smell of Italian. "Just relax."

She rolled her eyes and sat on the couch. She wasn't one for lounging around, but getting to watch Bjørn prepare their lunch might just make her okay with being lazy. He moved around the small kitchen with an efficiency that told how comfortable he was there. So, he flew choppers and could cook? A man in the kitchen had never been more attractive to her.

Reggie and Rowdy barreled down the stairs she assumed lead to the bedrooms. Their tongues hung out the side of their mouths, and their tails wagged. That Bjørn didn't care the dogs were running wild through his house made her draw to him even stronger. She thought of begging to God to make it work out between them but knew it'd be a wasted prayer. If she couldn't get past her scars, what made her think Bjørn would?

Bjørn sauntered to the couch, carrying two bowls of spaghetti. He handed her one with a flourish, and she noticed he gave her the bowl with more meatballs. She swallowed, unsure if she'd be able to eat with her stomach in a riot of chaotic butterflies.

"This looks amazing." She smiled as he sat down next to her. "Thanks."

"It's my ma's recipe." He shrugged and dug his fork into his bowl. "Mine isn't as good as hers, but it'll pass."

She shook her head as she stabbed at her food. He didn't just cook. He did it from scratch. Her culinary capabilities comprised of opening boxes and following directions. Most of the time, she didn't even do that, instead relying on Denali or the local restaurants to feed her.

Rowdy rushed up to her side and nosed her hands. The bowl of oozy sauce flipped from her grip before she could react and landed with a splat on her sweatshirt. It slid down the front of her, and she caught it before it could get all over the couch.

"Rowdy!" She gasped and pushed him away.

"I'll grab paper towels." Bjørn dashed to the kitchen, setting his bowl on the kitchen table as he passed.

Sadie took a deep breath and stood, leaning forward and letting the gloppy mess slide back into the bowl. Handing Bjørn the bowl as he gave her the paper towels, she cringed at the red sauce smeared down her front. She sighed. There went another shirt to the rag pile.

"I have some stain remover that's amazing." Bjørn grabbed the used paper towels and tossed them into the trash. "If we throw your sweatshirt in the washer now before the stain sets, you might be able to save it."

She froze, her breath catching in her throat. If she took off her sweatshirt, he'd see her scars. Then this entire thing between them would be over before it barely got off the ground. She wasn't ready for it to end, but he'd know something was up if she didn't.

"Sadie, what's wrong?" He stepped around the coffee table and pushed her ponytail over her shoulder.

"It's ... I ..." She closed her eyes and blurted out the words before she could change her mind. "I have scars from the avalanche. I—I don't want you to see them."

He ran his hand across her shoulder and down her arm, squeezing her fingers with his. "I'm not afraid of a few scars." His warm breath blew across the skin on her neck and rose all the little hairs there.

She shook her head and looked down, her cheeks and ears hot with embarrassment. "They're not just some little scars. They're disgusting." She couldn't keep the hitch out of her voice.

"Trust me." He gave a little tug on her sleeve, and her heart galloped into her throat.

Though she didn't want to, she pulled her arms into her sweatshirt. Dread coated her tongue in a sickeningly sour taste. As she grabbed the bottom hem and inched the fabric up over her head, her arms shook so hard she knew Bjørn could feel it. She kept the bulk of the sweatshirt over her arms, closed her eyes, and angled her shoulder so he couldn't see the scar along her collarbone. Why couldn't she have worn a T-shirt instead of the tank top? Then she could keep some of her scars hidden.

He feathered a kiss on the exposed skin of her shoulder. She gulped in a breath and held it. His next kiss branded her just below her ear, and she curled her toes as heat spread through her body. Showing him her arms was dangerous. It would cool all the sensations racing through her body like a dip in Resurrection Bay's ice-cold waters.

"Please, let me help you." Bjørn gave her a kiss on the jawbone, his palm cupping the back of her neck as he pulled away.

The desperation in his voice didn't escape her, like her pain somehow affected him. She opened her eyes and turned to look at him. She wasn't sure what expression she expected to see, but his unwavering eye contact and calm, even breaths pushed her to stop hiding. Giving him a quick nod, she sucked in a breath and pulled her arms the rest of the way out of her sweatshirt, handing the fabric to him.

Like two magnets drawn together, her gaze snapped to her puckered skin. Tears filled her vision and disgust closed her throat. She turned her head away, closing her eyes as a tear tracked down her cheek. The soft touch of fingers starting at her wrist and working their way up almost made her throw up.

"How did an avalanche do this?" He shifted next to her, his hand reaching for her other arm.

"When the snow hit the cabin, it pushed me into the wood stove before shoving me to the other side of the room." She squeezed her eyes even tighter with the memory of the burning pain. She touched her collarbone, then dropped her hand. "Thankfully, I can hide the ugly things, and it didn't get my face." Her bitter laugh filled her with shame. "So selfish. I'd take hideous scars all over if it meant Melinda was still here."

He lifted her arm up and pressed a kiss where molted skin started on the inside of her wrist. Flinching, she tried to pull away, but his gentle, yet firm hold on her stilled her. He slid one hand up her arm to cup her elbow and kissed the inside of the bend in her arm. The bitter taste in her mouth balled to a solid stone, making it hard to swallow.

"Don't ... I—" Her skin tingled at his touch, but it wasn't the crawling sensation of disgust. Another tear raced down her cheek. "Please. Sto—" The word cut short with another kiss where the burn was the deepest. "They're ugly." She choked out the words. How could he not see that? He shook his head as he ran his hand over them, really looking at them like he was gazing at a masterpiece.

"You're wrong, Sadie." He brought her wrist up so she could see and placed another kiss on top of the first. "Scars aren't ugly. They're beautiful reminders that you embrace life to the fullest, hit trials and hardships, and survived."

He peered at her, and she swore he looked straight into her soul. She swallowed, her heart pounding so hard in her chest it was about to burst out. Did he really mean that?

"You can't get scars while staying in safety." He leaned forward, pressing his lips to the wrinkled skin on her collarbone next to her shoulder.

Joy and doubt warred within, threatening to overwhelm her. So many people had cowered with one look at her skin. Most of the time, she couldn't stomach looking at it. He trailed his lips along her collarbone and up her neck toward her mouth, spiraling hope in hot waves straight to her heart. Bjørn's declaration settled beneath her skin as she placed her palms on his shoulders.

He stopped, his lips hovering a millimeter away. His choppy breaths mingled with hers, loud in her ears. She shivered. Not from cold, but from the desperation for what he said to be true.

"I wish you could see what I see." His lips brushed against hers. "You're so amazing. So gorgeous, both inside and out. You're—"

She captured his lips with hers, wrapping her arms around his neck as her entire body sparked to life. His hands bunched the back of her tank, then spread wide as he pulled her closer. She angled her head, deepening the kiss. She'd finally found someone who not only saw beyond her scars, but found beauty in them.

If Bjørn could look at her and see something wonderful, maybe she could too. She'd just have to hold tight to Bjørn's words, repeating them in her head until she believed them. He pulled the rubber band from her ponytail and threaded his fingers through her hair with a sigh as he kissed along her neck. If he kept kissing her like this, she might not have to repeat his words after all.

Chapter Fourteen

SADIE WHISTLED for Rowdy as he raced across the park's grass with Denali's Belgian Malinois, Hank. Pulling on the front of her sweatshirt to fan herself, the temptation to pant grew with each minute she was out in the summer heat. It was cold just half an hour before when the sun hid behind the clouds. It'd be nice if the Alaskan weather would just pick a temperature and stay there.

At this rate, she'd be a sweaty, stinky mess when they finished filming. Good thing smell-o-vision hadn't been invented yet.

Drew and his crew were busy setting up the cameras for their next training exercise. She'd come by earlier and buried a hat deep in the wood chips at the playground, and a baggie of synthetic narcotics several yards from the hat, under a tree.

The plan was to let Hank smell the gloves that went with the hat and Rowdy to smell the bag with the narcotic scent. They were hoping to show how the dogs could both find the item, even though they were being trained for different purposes. That a dog could be taught to find whatever the trainer had them smell, not just focusing on one thing.

This would be the first time they had tried this technique. She prayed it didn't flop like the training at the glacier the day before. Thinking of yesterday brought Bjørn rushing back to consume her thoughts. Not that he'd ever really left them. She'd spent most of the night replaying the day in her mind, marveling anew every time she went over Bjørn's words. She hoped the dark circles under her eyes from not being able to sleep didn't look horrible on the screen.

"What are you smiling like the Cheshire cat for?" Denali pushed against Sadie's shoulder, startling her.

She hadn't heard her cousin approaching. How long had Sadie stood there with a ridiculous smile on her face? She toned the expression down, but couldn't hide it completely.

Shrugging, she scanned the park to make sure Rowdy hadn't gone too far while she zoned out. "No reason."

"Hmm." Denali stared at Sadie, making her twitch under the scrutiny. "Aurora said Bjørn set up a training hide and seek for you. Did you find him?"

Did she ever. Sadie's neck heated in a blush. She puckered her lips and blew a two-tone sound that signaled Rowdy to come.

"Yeah. I found him." Sadie crouched as Rowdy came up to her and rubbed his face.

"You got home pretty late last night." Denali crossed her arms.

Sadie's ears turned blazing hot under her cousin's scrutiny.

"I knew it." Denali poked Sadie's shoulder. "Something happened between you two. Now spill it."

Sadie bit her lip, then stood and stepped close to Denali. "It was amazing. He's amazing." Her gaze dashed around to make sure Drew was still setting up. "Bjørn hid in a glacier crevasse, and I had a panic attack while searching."

"That's amazing?" Denali's eyebrow rose in skepticism.

"No, that was embarrassing." Sadie plowed on, her hands flying as she spoke. "But he talked me through it and didn't decide I was some lost cause. We went back to his place to have lunch and watch a movie." She grabbed Denali's arm. "Did you know he lives right down the street from us?"

"No." Denali laughed, her smile the one she gave Sadie when she was telling one of her wild stories.

"Yep. Cute place," Sadie said. "Anyway, he brings me a bowl of homemade spaghetti and meatballs."

"He cooks?" Denali interrupted.

Sadie nodded. She cringed with the memory and told Denali how Rowdy spilled the spaghetti. Denali covered her mouth with her hand.

"What did you do?" Denali's amused look turned to concern as she lowered her hand from her mouth. She knew just how self-conscious Sadie was about the scars.

Sadie stared off into the distance. Awe still flowed through her with Bjørn's push to help her. "He asked me to trust him, so I took off the sweatshirt." She shook her head, pulling her back. "He would find out eventually, so I figured I might as well get it over with."

"What'd he do when he saw them?" Denali's voice held caution.

"He kissed them. Told me they spoke of my strength." Sadie's throat hurt with happy tears. "Called them beautiful. Called *me* beautiful."

"That's because you are." Denali threaded her fingers through Sadie's and shook her hand. "Always have been."

"I think he's the one." Sadie shrugged as a tear breached her lashes and dashed down her cheek. "I know it's crazy, and I might get my heart broken, but I just—"

"Everything okay over here?" Drew walked up from behind them, and Sadie swiped her cheek.

"Yep. Everything's great." Denali rolled her eyes. Poor Drew had his work cut out for him with her. "Just like a guy to interrupt when the story was getting good," she muttered under her breath before calling for Hank.

"We're ready whenever you are." Drew pointed his thumb toward the cameras. His gaze darted between Sadie and Denali before he held his hands up at his sides in a move of surrender. "No rush, though."

"We're ready." Sadie bumped her shoulder against Denali's and whispered. "Be nice."

"Not guaranteeing anything," Denali said with a grumble.

"Rowdy!" Sadie called and jogged toward the grassy section.

Another dog bolted from the bushes and ran toward them with a happy yip. He was a huge lab with his tongue hanging out of his mouth. A chuckle bubbled up from Sadie at how goofy he looked as he bounded to them. Rowdy wagged his back end, getting caught up in the excitement.

Sadie scanned the area the dog had come from.

Where was the big guy's owner? Sadie shifted course, pulling out her leash from her pocket just in case the dog didn't follow orders.

"Hey, big guy. Did you get loose?"

Sadie laughed as the lab and Rowdy circled each other, pawing at one another like they were long-lost friends. Their playing escalated, and they barreled into Sadie, knocking her on her back. The big lab stepped on her stomach, and her breath whooshed out of her with an *oomph*.

"Get off, you big lug." She pushed him off with a laugh before turning serious. "Rowdy, come."

Rowdy stopped his playing, his head snapping in her direction. Sadie pushed herself to her feet. Thank goodness her dog listened. She snapped her finger and pointed to her side. Rowdy's head hung as he made his way. The griffon breed was known for being sensitive. It was what made them so easy to train, but the way he'd get all sad that he had let her down always made her chuckle.

"You're not in trouble." She rubbed behind his ear. "You just have to learn not to run with the wild crowd."

A young woman ran up, her eyes wide on her petite face. "I am so sorry! Lovebug got away from me again."

"Lovebug?" Drew choked out a laugh as he stepped up beside Sadie.

"He's such a tank." The woman's expression turned from worry to exasperation. "I can't get him to listen."

Sadie bit the inside of her cheek to keep her retort in. The lady probably never trained the dog to begin with. Her eyes filled with tears as she tried to call Lovebug over. Sadie stuffed down her annoyance.

"We rarely do pet training, but if you call North

STAR Kennel, we can set up some classes for you and Lovebug." Sadie rubbed her aching belly where the monster dog had stepped.

"You'd do that?" the lady asked with surprise.

"Yeah, sure." Sadie shrugged.

"Oh, thank you!" Lovebug's owner threw her arms around Sadie only to jump back, her face scrunched in disgust as she looked at her hands covered in brown poo.

"Oh no." The rank smell hit Sadie as she twisted to see the back of her sweatshirt.

Drew stepped away and waved his hand in front of his face. "Mate, that's a smelly one."

"Great." Sadie's armpits started to sweat even more.

"I'm so sorry." The lady wiped her hands on the grass and snagged Lovebug's collar as he attacked her with kisses while she bent down.

"Don't worry about it." Sadie waved her off. "It'll wash out."

"I'm just going to get this big lug home before he does any more damage." The lady dragged Lovebug off.

"Do we need to wait to film, or are you good to go?" Drew tipped his head toward the cameramen approaching.

"We're good, just …" Sadie wanted to throw the stupid shirt off and not worry about her scars, but she wasn't ready for that yet. "Just give me a minute."

"No worries. Take your time," Drew said before going to his cameramen.

Denali gave her a small nod and an encouraging smile. "Just remember what Bjørn said."

Sadie took a deep breath and yanked the sweatshirt off, being careful not to get any poop in her hair. Cool air hit her skin, and she sighed in relief. Pulling the fabric the rest of the way off her arms, she tossed the shirt next to a tree.

Bands tightened around her chest as she turned to Drew and his crew. She hated that their reaction meant so much, but it did. Maybe someday it wouldn't. Denali stared at Drew from the side, her arms crossed, ready for a confrontation.

Drew's gaze skimmed from Sadie's shoulder to her arms, one eyebrow rising as he met her eyes. "You ready?"

What? No reaction or questions about how she got the scars? Denali's arms dropped as her expression turned from mama-bear protective to surprise.

"I'm ready." Sadie stepped up to Denali and pushed her arm to snap her out of her shock. "Let's see what our dogs can do."

Chapter Fifteen

"Man, Gunnar, I'm telling you, Sadie is amazing." Bjørn pulled a soda out of Gunnar's fridge and popped the tab.

"I know." Gunnar grumbled from the kitchen table. "It's all you've talked about since you got here." He glanced at his watch. "Two hours ago."

"Whatever." Bjørn took a deep drink. The carbonation bubbled down his throat, adding its pop to his already excited nerves. "And it's not all I've talked about."

Gunnar didn't say a word, just raised one eyebrow. He twirled his pen between his fingers, then tapped it on the table.

"Okay, sorry. I'll focus." Bjørn sat down with a huff and shifted the papers around in front of him. "It's just that I'm not sure where to go from here with her."

Gunnar pushed back from the table with a groan and threw the pen onto the papers. "We aren't getting anything done, so talk."

"Man, I don't know. Like, I think she's the one."

Bjørn pushed his hand through his hair as his neck heated. He sounded like such an idiot. "It's crazy, and it all seems so fast. Is it possible to fall in love that quick, or is it just my need to check off the next thing on my list that's making me lift off without doing a safety check first?"

"It's possible." Gunnar looked at his hands as he open and closed them. "Happened with me when I met Julie. Though, I guess a little different. One minute we were just friends, then suddenly she was so much more."

Bjørn froze. Gunnar hadn't talked about his high school sweetheart and only love since he left home for basic. Bjørn understood why Gunnar broke things off with her before going into the Air Force. He had needed to concentrate to become a pararescueman. What Bjørn didn't understand was why Gunnar didn't at least see what Julie was up to now. He obviously still had feelings for her, from his lack of dating anyone since they broke up and her unopened letters he carried in his pack. Finding them while Bjørn had looked for a flashlight had surprised him so much he hadn't thought it smart to bring it up before. But now, all bets were off.

"You ever going to call her?" Bjørn's question dropped into the space like a well-placed grenade. The pause was deafening.

"No." Gunnar clenched his hands into fists and leaned his forearms on the chair's armrest. "I botched it." His gaze darted to his pack that he took everywhere, then down to the ground. Bjørn could almost feel the letters burning a hole through the material. "Probably married with kids. She doesn't need me asking to catch up over coffee."

"You never know. She might not have gotten

married." Bjørn hated that Gunnar thought there wasn't hope. "Wouldn't it be better to know than to always wonder?"

Gunnar shook his head. "I want her to be happy, but I'm not sure I could handle seeing it."

"But what if she's not?" Bjørn quickly continued when Gunnar's head snapped up and his face went all stormy. "I mean, what if she's not married, man? What if you could have a second chance with her?"

Gunnar shook his head and pushed off the chair, stomping to the kitchen. "We're talking about you here, not me. Let it go."

Bjørn wondered what it would be like to love someone as much as Gunnar obviously loved Julie but let her go for a greater cause. Is that what Bjørn would have to do with Sadie? Her father didn't want them together. If they continued dating, would Will kick Bjørn off the SAR team? Bjørn shook his head at his thoughts. He didn't think he could handle just flying tourists around. He needed to feel like he was helping, adding benefit to the community he called home.

"Sadie's dad found out about that mission Yancy botched and blamed on me." Bjørn rubbed his finger along the smooth wood of the table. "Doesn't want me helping Sadie with her training and the TV show."

"Your name got cleared," Gunnar called from the kitchen.

"Yeah, but not everyone knows that part." Frustration built in Bjørn's chest at the injustice. "They only remember the juicy gossip. Doesn't help that Will's cousin is brass in SOAR."

Gunnar grunted and turned the water on. Memories of the mission and months after ran through Bjørn's brain, filling it to the brim with the anger, hurt, and dismay that had overwhelmed him during those months of investigation. He thought he'd put all that behind him. Guess he still had work to do on that end.

"Don't worry." Gunnar set his glass of water on the table with a clunk and sat. "The truth will surface."

"Yeah." Bjørn sank against the back of his chair with a sigh. "What should I do about Sadie? I mean, I'm out here to go over our business stuff, and all I can think about is calling to see how the shoot went. I'm like flying without instruments here. Should I power down or go ahead and lift off?"

Thirty-one years old, and he felt like a teenager with his first crush. He shouldn't need his older brother to tell him what to do. He'd flown with SOAR as one of their top pilots, for Pete's sake. He could handle pressure … unless it came to a certain brown-eyed woman who tackled life headfirst and had the scars to prove it.

Gunnar snorted. "Go call her. Don't screw up like I did." He crossed his arms over his chest. "Be ready to work when you're done."

"Yes, sir." Bjørn saluted and rushed out to the front porch.

Pulling up her contact on his phone, his mouth stretched into a goofy smile he couldn't contain, and his heart pounded in his chest like he was firing a Vulcan M134. His shoes slapped hard against the wood planks of the porch as he paced back and forth while the phone rang on and on. She must still be busy. He stopped, his shoulders drooping as he prepared to leave a message.

"Hello? Bjørn?" Sadie's out of breath voice had his insides jumping like he was a six-year-old hopped up on sugar.

"Hey, beautiful." He leaned against the railing as his world suddenly righted and he could think straight. Oh, this was bad. It was like she was a drug, and he was addicted.

Her soft laugh settled warmth in his stomach. "What are you up to?"

"Trying to hammer out some details of blending mine and Gunnar's businesses." Bjørn crossed his ankles and smiled. "You know, list stuff."

"No." Her mock gasp had him chuckling. "You're making lists?"

"Trying to." He pushed off the railing and meandered toward his truck.

"It's not going well?" All joking left her voice to be replaced with concern.

Man, she was something else. A firecracker full of life, dreams, and energy all precariously balanced like spinning plates, yet willing to add another to help someone else. He might as well pack her up and take her to meet Ma and Dad, because he was taking Gunnar's advice and letting this relationship soar.

"Well, I can't seem to stop thinking about a certain dog trainer I know long enough to get any work done." He kicked his tire, a little nervous about what she'd say.

"Is that so?" Her amusement was tinged with a breathlessness that injected him with boldness.

"I miss you." He leaned his back against his truck and stared off toward the jagged mountains.

"I miss you too."

Her low, throaty whisper made him wish he could pull her close, run his fingers through her hair, and kiss her senseless. He had to focus and get some work done. If he could convince her to let him cook her dinner, he'd greet her with all the pent-up energy thoughts of her had created with a kiss she'd remember.

He cleared his throat. "I wanted to see how the shoot went."

"It went amazing." Her joy rushed through the phone, and he could picture her hands swinging wide with excitement. "I got barreled over by this rogue dog named Lovebug and landed in an enormous pile of poo."

"Okay." He shook his head with a laugh, not seeing how that could be amazing.

"Well, that wasn't great. Disgusting, actually." She took a breath so deep and loud he could hear it through the phone. "I didn't have time to go home and change, so I either had to do the shoot with poop smeared all down my back or take off my sweatshirt."

Bjørn's throat got tight. From what she'd said the day before, she never let anyone see her scars. That must've been horrible for her.

"Bjørn, no one cared about my scars." Shock filled her voice. "They barely gave them a second glance."

Bjørn closed his eyes and sagged against the hot metal. He'd told her the truth the day before when he said her scars were beautiful, but people could sometimes look on just the outside without seeing past the skin. He never imagined he'd feel such relief to hear her confidence in herself.

"That's because they aren't that bad, and those whose opinions matter know what an amazing person you are." He prayed her experiences showing her scars continued to be as uplifting as they'd been so far. "So, my TV starlet …" He smiled as she snorted. "Do you have any plans tonight?"

"That depends." Her tone turned all coy-like, and his heart about burst from his chest. "There's this chopper pilot that I'm hoping to see. Real nice guy. I think you'd like him."

"Unless you're talking about me, I'd hate him." Bjørn pushed off from the truck and meandered to the house. "What if I make you dinner, and we go for a walk along the Lost Lake Trail afterwards?"

"That sounds perfect. Does six work?"

"I'll be ready. I can't wait to see you." Bjørn needed to get his work done with Gunnar so he could run by the store and get home.

"Me too. I gotta go. The puppies got loose. Bye." Sadie hollered, and the call cut off.

Bjørn stared at his phone, a lightness filling him like helium, replacing the anxiousness of earlier. He shoved it into his pocket and whistled the rest of the way to the house. Now that things were going great with Sadie, he just needed to find a way to get Will to see that Bjørn could be depended on.

His steps slowed as he pulled open the front door. With Will's cousin, a decorated officer of the Air Force, spreading rumors about Bjørn, that might be a tough mission. He pressed his lips together as a headache formed. He didn't want to fight the battle for his reputation that botched mission had created again. Wasn't once enough?

Chapter Sixteen

SADIE PULLED up to the airstrip the next day, still on a high from her date with Bjørn the night before. Even her dad's continued resistance to them dating, even after she had talked to him, couldn't bring her down. She'd just have to keep trying to convince her dad that Bjørn could be trusted.

Who knew dinner and a walk along the trail could be so romantic? They'd walked late into the night, the midnight sun making it seem earlier than it was. When they'd finally gotten back to his place, it had shocked her it was already one in the morning. Time seemed to have no bearing when she was with Bjørn. She rubbed her lips with her fingers. She'd definitely been dating the wrong men.

Turning into the parking spot next to Bjørn's truck, she chugged the last of her Mexican mocha from The Rez, got out of the Land Cruiser, and motioned for Rowdy to follow. Bjørn came around the front of his helicopter with a clipboard in hand, bending and checking things for preflight. When Rowdy yipped a joyful sound and took off across the asphalt, Bjørn's head snapped up. Sadie could see his smile across the distance, and the thought that she put it there made her body tingle from head to toe.

She grabbed her pack from the backseat and locked the door. "Keep yourself together, girl." She muttered through her smile. "No need to run up like Rowdy, body all wiggling, and throw yourself at the man."

Bjørn tossed his clipboard into the chopper, then sauntered toward her, closing the distance with sure, even strides. His intense gaze never left her face. She wiped her sweaty palms on her pants and resisted the urge to cross her bare arms over her chest. She still wasn't comfortable with her scars uncovered.

He didn't stop until he was right up on her, wrapping his arms around her waist and pulling her close. His lips captured hers with a hunger that zinged electric heat from her scalp to her fingertips. She dropped her pack to the ground and wrapped her arms around his shoulders. She never wanted to let go. Prayed reality wouldn't crash in.

"Hey." His lips fluttered against hers.

"Hi." She managed to force the word past the hard pounding of her heart in her throat.

He slid his hands up her back and along her arms. The roughness of his palms against her skin raised the hairs on the back of her neck and raced delicious shivers to her toes. He kissed the inside of her right elbow just at the start of her scars, and her knees threatened to buckle. He smiled like he knew he turned her to mush, pressed his lips to the inside of her wrist, then threaded his fingers through hers.

"You ready for another training episode?" He

grabbed her bag from the ground and pulled her toward the chopper.

The honk of a horn behind her startled a squeak from her. She spun to look as Drew pulled the network's van next to hers. How hadn't she heard him drive up? She glanced around, wondering what else had happened while Bjørn obliterated her mind. He shook her hand and squeezed. His eyebrow rose in question.

"Huh?" Her forehead scrunched as she tried to remember what he'd asked, and his smile turned cocky. She glared and pushed him away as her face heated, but he held on tight to her hand.

"I like that I rattle you." He moved their joined hands behind her back and pulled her close. "I missed you."

She snorted, though her heart leaped with joy like a spastic border collie. "It's been less than eight hours."

"Too long." His kiss was quick but still left her lips tingling. "Looks like Rowdy is ready."

She followed Bjørn's gaze to where Rowdy waited in the chopper. When the silly dog saw the two of them looking at him, his ears tucked back and his entire body wiggled. He turned, searching for something in the helicopter, and came back to the edge of the door with a pair of earmuffs in his mouth. She tipped her head back and laughed.

Her phone buzzed in her pocket. She let out a groan when her dad's face looked at her from the screen. Her talk with him this morning hadn't gone any better than the other night at the restaurant. Disappointing him had never been an option for her growing up, and doing so now went against who she'd always been. Violet bucked and challenged their parents, not Sadie … until now.

"Hey, Dad." She smiled at Bjørn as he squeezed her hand and let go.

"Where are you?" Dad's voice fired through the phone.

No hello. No apology. Just those curt, three words.

"Getting ready to film another episode." The nerves flipping like a salmon in her stomach threatened to push the lemon scone and mocha out.

"Denali said you're with Bjørn." Her dad's tone was thick with disapproval. Why did her dad have to make an issue of this?

"Yeah." She crossed her arms to protect herself from what he'd say next.

"He there?"

"Yeah." The fish flipped up her esophagus, and she swallowed.

"Put me on speaker." His order had her sweating.

"I don't think that's a good idea, Dad. I've talked to Bjørn about—"

"This isn't about that." His voice was still gruff, but she caught his urgency. "I need his—and your—help."

She pulled the phone away from her ear. With a shaky finger, she pressed the speaker icon as Drew walked up beside them. She inwardly begged her dad not to say anything rude or that would shine a poor light on Bjørn. Bjørn's eyebrow rose as he looked at her.

"Okay, you're on speaker." Sadie sucked in a breath and held it.

"I'm glad I caught you." Dad's relief was not what she was expecting. "We have some missing teens and need you to fly out and search for them."

"Okay." She cringed at Drew and mouthed, "Sorry."

She turned to Bjørn, holding the phone closer to him. "Where are they?"

"They took a boat into the bay to hike into Eshamy Lake." Dad rattled off the information. "They never called in, and a report from a pilot that flew over the area this morning said he didn't see a boat anywhere near."

"What kind of watercraft did they take?" Bjørn asked as he pulled out a map from the chopper.

"They're in a white Intrepid Powerboat with the hillsides painted red." Dad sighed.

Bjørn whistled in appreciation, but Sadie didn't have a clue what that meant.

"That's a fancy boat for teens to be taking out." Bjørn studied the map. "Who else do you have looking?"

"You're it, at the moment. I'm hoping to round up another plane or two, and I'll be heading out in my speedboat as soon as I make a few more calls." Dad's voice muffled as he spoke to someone else, then came back to them. "I know this messes up your nature show."

"Actually, it'll be perfect," Drew chimed in. "Having these rescue missions will just make the show even better. The execs went nuts over the last one we filmed."

"I don't think it's a good idea." Dad's tone turned hard. "Sadie, it's the Miller boy, and you know how his family can get."

Sadie wrung her hands as anxiety settled like a boulder in her chest. There were a million Millers in the world, but she knew exactly who her dad was talking about. They thought the wealth they'd accumulated entitled them to be treated better than others and were constantly causing issues in the community.

Could she go against her dad again? Her heart shrank in her chest at the thought of letting him down. She was twenty-seven, for Pete's sake. Shouldn't she be past feeling the dread of disappointing her parents?

She blew out a breath as she stared at Drew. He brought his clasped hands up to his face and begged like a five-year-old.

Her dad was going to kill her.

"Dad, we need Drew and his team along to help search." Sadie bit her lower lip as her wheels turned for the right words to say. "We can't afford to wait for more people to show up. Besides, the cameramen are good at using their observation skills, otherwise Nature wouldn't be winning all these awards for their documentaries."

"We'll leave the cameras in the chopper when we find them. Just video the take off and flying out of the bay, sir, then we'll all focus on the job at hand," Drew added.

"Sadie." Dad didn't sound convinced.

"Gotta go." She tipped her head toward the chopper, motioning for Drew to load up. "We'll keep in contact."

She hung up and shoved the phone back in her pocket. Dad was going to be livid she was going against him yet again. She closed her eyes as guilt slicked over her in muggy heat. He'd come around. He had to.

Bjørn kissed her on the cheek, then moved around the chopper. She followed him with her eyes, his quick agreement to drop everything to help someone else replacing the guilt with hope ... with love. If her dad never came around, would she be able to live with his disappointment? What if he went so far that he stopped speaking to her? The thought twisted in her heart.

Family meant everything to her, but what she had with Bjørn was special too. She wasn't sure if she could choose between Bjørn or her family.

Bjørn scanned the coastline before him again, hoping that he'd see the boat tucked within a cove. Nothing. Breathing out a calming breath, he checked his gauges, running through his safety checklists to slow his heart rate. He'd learned that trick as a pilot for SOAR. Keeping a level head was the only way to get through a mission, especially one that falls apart.

He leaned forward and tipped his gaze to the mountaintops. The clouds hanging low had inched closer to the ocean. His heart sank. They didn't have much time before the fog set in.

He turned to Sadie in the copilot seat. His lips tipped up at how adorable she looked with the big headset on and her forehead scrunched in concern. He loved how she could switch from playful to all business with just a word. Life with her wouldn't be boring.

Worry pooled in his gut as he stared at her. She'd gone against her father again. Sure, she was old enough to make her own decisions and directions in life, but he gathered from her comments and stories she'd shared that disappointing her parents—disappointing anyone—went against her nature. She had dreams and did everything she could to achieve them, but she was also a people pleaser. She definitely wasn't pleasing her father now, not with her continuing to see Bjørn and now bringing the TV crew along.

"See anything?" he asked before his brain wandered

off in daydreams. So unlike him, but since meeting Sadie, it'd become a recurring condition.

"No." Her shoulders slumped as she turned to the guys in the back. "What about back there?"

"Nothing," Drew said. "The fog is closing in pretty fast too."

"Yeah." Sadie rubbed Rowdy's head where it lay between the seats and turned forward. "We need the sun to break back through."

Bjørn shook his head as he pulled on Rowdy's soft ear. The dog leaned into the pet, his tongue hanging out. He truly was a super dog, taking to flying like he'd been doing it since birth. He never once got nervous, and Bjørn wondered if it was the training Sadie had put him through as a puppy or if he really was just that chill. Whatever the reason, the more Bjørn was around the dog, the more he wanted a griffon. Of course, if he married Sadie, he wouldn't have to get one of his own.

He snapped his attention back to the scenery before him. He was getting way ahead of his action plan. Jumping to the tenth step wouldn't get him to the end any quicker.

"Rebel, this is Chief. Come back with an update. Over." Will's voice broke through the radio like he'd read Bjørn's mind and wanted to shake him up.

"Chief, this is Rebel. We've gone all along this coast. No sign of the boat or the occupants. Over."

Bjørn peeked back up at the fog tumbling down the mountain like some giant blew it toward them. The windshield slicked wet with dew, and the air in the chopper turned cold. Bjørn flipped some switches, turning up the heater and the wipers.

"We're coming up empty here too." Weariness hung

in Will's voice and mirrored Bjørn's own feelings. "Weather is rolling in. I want everyone to head back to base. We'll get updates and come up with a plan for when the weather clears enough to go back out."

Bjørn shook his head, not willing to give up yet. The air grew thick around them, making it hard to see, but he could still make out shapes. What if the kids were just around the next bend?

"Negative. We can keep going." Bjørn ignored Sadie as her head snapped his direction.

"Rebel, I know you like to showboat, but this fog is just going to get thicker," Will said. "I don't want to have to save you as well. Turn back to Seward. That's an order."

The atmosphere in the chopper stilled, like everyone held their breath to see what Bjørn would do. He glanced along the shoreline and clenched his teeth in agitation. Did he want to stay out despite visibility decreasing with each second because he was confident in his ability or to prove he wasn't the man rumors made him out to be? A gust of wind shuddered the chopper, pushing more soupy clouds over them.

"Rebel?" Will's sharp voice punctured Bjørn's indecision.

"Copy that." Bjørn's cheek muscle clicked in frustration. "Rebel coming home."

The air in the cabin heaved like a collective sigh. Bjørn turned his head away from Sadie and scanned one last time out the window to hide his disappointment. He hated the thought of teens out there somewhere, possibly hurt, and rescue not coming. Hated that it brought up the memories of the mission that had tainted his military career. He also knew it wouldn't do his team any good to stay out there burning fuel when they couldn't see past the rotors.

"We'll come back out as soon as the fog clears." Sadie's hand rested on his shoulder. "This will give us a chance to rest, regroup, and hopefully get more help."

He touched her hand upon his shoulder and gave it a squeeze. Was she worried about seeing her dad? Would Will hold it against her that she let the TV crew tag along? Bjørn hoped not. They had needed the crew's eyes to help search. Bjørn would back her until he was blue in the face if he had to. With a nod and a sinking feeling in his gut, he turned the bird and pointed her nose toward home.

Chapter Seventeen

SADIE RUBBED her fingers against edge of her T-shirt sleeve as she listened to her dad break down the rescue mission plan. The stuffy room was crowded with community members, family of the teens, and other SAR teams from around the state. The people pressed in on her, making her palms clammy and her heart race. The only thing that kept her sitting on the table was the kids needing help and Bjørn sitting next to her. Otherwise, she would probably have made a beeline for the door before the meeting had even started.

She wished her dad had moved to a bigger location so the room wouldn't be so crowded. She brushed her shaky hands against her pants to wipe the sweat from them. Scanning the room, her gaze snagged on her ex-boyfriend, Leo, casually lounging against a table on the opposite side. He stared at her across the packed space, his lips curled up in an amused smirk. He'd been doing that the entire meeting. Catching her eye, his expression twisted in cruel humor. Why she'd ever found him attractive was beyond her.

He leaned to the person sitting next to him, whispered something, then jutted his chin toward her. His friend glanced across the room, then shrugged. Sadie jerked, her hands balling into fists on her lap. Bjørn's head turned her way, so she tore her gaze away from Leo.

"You okay?" Bjørn leaned over and whispered, placing his hand over hers. His gaze darted across the room.

She forced a smile and nodded, crossing her arms over her chest. Forehead wrinkling in concern, he stared at her for a moment before turning his attention back to her dad. She wanted to lean up against him and soak in his strength, to take his hand in hers so her nerves would fire on alert for a reason other than fear. With her father's disapproval hanging over her for the TV crew going on the mission, she didn't want to push herself even further into the doghouse by clinging to Bjørn in front of her dad. He'd eventually have to get used to seeing her with Bjørn, but she didn't need to flaunt it when he was under the pressure of the search.

"What I want to know is why you called off the search when you had a team willing to keep going?" Mr. Miller cut off her dad's breakdown.

"Jim, you know how the fog can set in." Dad's low voice held a hint of exasperation. "Our team would've had zero visibility. It's too dangerous to be flying in that."

"You can't possibly know that." Jim waved his hands in the air, his face turning redder with each word. "This Rebel guy could've found my son by now if you hadn't called them back. Do you even know what you're doing?"

Bjørn shifted beside Sadie, his hands clenching on the table's edge they sat on. How did Jim even know what Bjørn had said? He must've been listening in on the radio frequency. Sadie swallowed down the apprehension that built in her throat and stared at her dad. Jim was known for causing a ruckus. Would he create a problem for Dad just to get his way? Sadie took a deep breath and began praying for her dad. Jim would most definitely cause issues. It was what he excelled at.

He scanned the room, and Sadie tried to shrink from his searching. His eyes landed on Drew's TV crew and narrowed. Oh, no. Sadie's eyes widened as they darted to her dad. He looked at her, his cheek flexing, before he turned his focus back on Jim.

"And another thing." Jim waved to Bo and Craig at the back of the room. "When did SAR turn into a reality TV show?" Jim's words had Bo and Craig straightening in their chairs. "You'll push your family's agenda but won't stay out there and look for our kids?"

Drew slid off the table next to Bjørn and stepped forward. "I assure you, my crew spent hours scanning the terrain for signs of those kids. Every single one of us has training in first aid and has extensive experience in the wild." Drew's comments eased some of her nervousness. "Nothing matters more to us than finding these teens."

Jim's wife pulled on his hand for him to sit down, but he yanked it free. "I want my kid found, whatever the cost."

Ice slid down Sadie's back. She wanted to believe that it was worry pushing his words, but from his past, she knew better. He didn't care about other people, only about what benefitted him, which at the moment was them finding his son. He sat with a huff in his chair and crossed his arms.

Dad dropped his hands to his sides and widened his stance. "Okay. You all have your areas. Keep base updated with what you find."

He turned to the table behind him and gathered up his stuff. Sadie had to get out of there before people started milling about and closed the space even smaller. Hopping from the table, she walked as fast as she could for the door without actually running. She burst from the building and sucked in a deep breath before stomping toward her vehicle. She needed to swing by the kennel to pick up Rowdy before she headed to the airstrip.

A hand grabbed her elbow and jerked her around. Leo sneered, stepped back, and wiped his hand on his pants like touching her made him dirty. She lifted her eyebrow, resisting the urge to cross her arms to hide her scars.

"Running to hide?" He drew out the words in a taunt as he looked pointedly at her arms.

"What do you want, Leo?" She really didn't care.

Bjørn stepped out of the building behind Leo, his forehead scrunching when he saw her. Reporters hollered and rushed up to him. She hoped he'd blow them off and come up to her. Maybe then Leo would leave her alone. Leo followed her gaze, then turned back with a flush on his face.

"Looks like you've finally landed yourself a date." Leo stepped closer. "I think I could be convinced to date you if it came with a TV endorsement too."

She stepped back, cocking her head to the side at what he just said. He thought Bjørn was with her for the show. Her gaze darted to where he spoke with the reporters. The reporters hadn't questioned anyone else, had they?

An unkind smile spread across Leo's face as closed the distance between them and rubbed his hand down her arm. "I might even let you show these ugly arms if it meant people would flock to me." He leaned in and whispered, "Everyone loves a sob story."

Her mouth dropped open, and she stepped back from him, turning her left side to him. She needed to leave before she did something she'd regret in front of the reporters.

He tipped his head to the reporters. "But they love the hero even better."

White hot anger coursed from her chest. She threw a jab at his face with her left arm. His eyes widened as he dodged away from the punch, straight into her right cross. Pain exploded up her arm as her fist connected with his face. Satisfaction quickly replaced the pain as Leo stumbled back and fell to the ground with blood spurting over his mouth. Her dad's hello and goodbye punch sequence he'd drilled into them had actually worked.

"You broke my nose!" Leo glared up from the cement.

"You said you wanted publicity." She shook out her hand. "Go sob to someone who cares."

She peeked up at Bjørn. He hadn't moved, hadn't come to her rescue, but an amused smile stretched across his face. She didn't need a white knight to rush in and save her, but it sure would've been nice if he'd tried. All the reporters froze, their eyes bouncing between her and Leo like they were just waiting for something even juicier to jump on.

Sadie spun on her heels and stomped to her vehicle. She flexed her throbbing fingers and pressed her lips tight together as her heart shrank in her chest. She clenched her teeth and sniffled. She had work to do and kids to find.

Chapter Eighteen

BJØRN AMBLED after Sadie as she rushed from the meeting, shooting off a text to Gunnar that they were heading to the airstrip and to join them. She'd been on edge the entire time. But he didn't think it just had to do with the closed-in space. Who was that jerk that had been staring at her from across the room? Bjørn had kept his hands wrapped around the table's edge so he didn't drape his arm across her shoulder in a caveman claim and stare the man down.

Between the tension stretching from Sadie to the guy and then the father of the missing kid pulling Bjørn into the heat of the fire, he had spent the meeting with a heavy lump of dread weighing in his gut. He sighed as he pushed out the doors into fresh air. He'd be surprised if Will Wilde ever changed his opinion of Bjørn.

Reporters barreled toward him, hollering his name, and he pulled up short. He didn't need this right now. He had to grab more supplies from his place and get the chopper ready to fly. The last thing he wanted was for a camera to be shoved in his face while people peppered questions at him.

"Captain Rebel, Katie Cullens with KTUU. You've flown dangerous missions for the military into every conceivable circumstance." A pretty reporter shoved her way to the front, and Bjørn chewed the inside of his cheek in frustration. "Could you have continued flying?"

Why hadn't Bjørn considered that people would listen to the radios? He hated that he had caused Will this scrutiny when he'd made the right call. Unease also slid beneath his skin that his service in the army was being pulled into the mix. His missions were all closed, top-secret stuff, but if a person dug in the right places, his reputation could crumble like it had before.

"The fog was thick and settled in quickly." Bjørn shoved his hands in his pockets as his gaze darted to Sadie and the guy from the meeting talking.

"So flying was impossible?" Katie pressed.

"Not impossible, but definitely not safe." Bjørn's attention veered back to Sadie as the man took her elbow, her expression turning hard as she glanced to Bjørn. He should go to her.

"Some are wondering if Will Wilde is the right person to be heading this search." Katie's statement pulled Bjørn back. "Do you think Will Wilde was right in calling off the search?"

The guy with Sadie stepped closer. Bjørn really needed to get over there, but he also wanted to clear up any confusion over Will and his ability to do his job. Sadie's mouth dropped open, then fury flashed across it. Her left fist swung toward the guy's head, followed perfectly by her right. Elation and pride volleyed in Bjørn's chest as the guy whined about his nose being broken. Bjørn didn't need to help her with the jerk, but he could help the Wildes with the hound dogs trying to sniff up trouble. He smiled at Sadie to show her his pride, then turned to the reporters to draw their attention away from the commotion.

"Katie, you want to know about Will Wilde?" He rubbed his hands together in front of him like he had a secret.

He let enough intrigue slip into his tone to reel them in. All the reporters turned to him, anticipation practically making them drool. Now he just needed to set the hook.

"Will Wilde was spot on in calling us home. I let my frustration with not finding the kids spill into our conversation, but if we'd stayed out there any longer, we would've had to find a place to land and wait out the fog. If we even could have done that." Bjørn easily could have, but the reporters didn't need to know that. "Will Wilde is an amazing commander with his finger on the pulse of this area. There isn't anyone that I've met that could do the job he does any better, and it's a privilege and an honor to work alongside him."

"But what of Mr. Miller's insistence that the search could've continued?" Katie shoved her microphone back in Bjørn's face, and his frustration with the delay turned to contempt at her ignorance of how dangerous these situations were.

"Mr. Miller is speaking out of worry for his son, which I understand, but Miller wasn't there." He widened his stance as he shook his head, trying to keep his words from exploding out of him and making things worse. "The fog became thick as soup with zero visibility. Wilde made the right call, bringing us back in to regroup. Now, if you'll excuse me. I can't do my part in finding these kids talking to you."

He pushed past them and headed toward his truck. His gait, stiff with agitation, jerked when he noticed Will standing behind the reporters with his arms crossed. He glanced behind Bjørn at the reporters, then back at Bjørn. Will's head tipped in thanks as the horde descended upon him with questions. Bjørn's steps to his truck were lighter than they'd been since they had touched down. If they could just find the kids, maybe Will's opinion of Bjørn would change completely.

Sadie slung her pack on and stomped up to the chopper. Her hand throbbed from smashing it into Leo's nose, and her emotions ran high at Bjørn's amusement of her fight. He came around the front of the bird, that same smile on his face. She flexed her fingers. She might just have to give him the ol' hello-goodbye greeting too.

"There's my slugger." Bjørn met her at the chopper's door.

Clenching her teeth, she tossed her bag in the back and motioned for Rowdy to load up. She couldn't look at Bjørn right now, not when she didn't know if she'd start bawling or punching. Maybe both.

"How's your hand?" Bjørn reached for her, and she jerked away. "Sadie?" His forehead wrinkled with confusion in her peripheral.

She glanced toward the airstrip road. Why couldn't the others be here, so she didn't have to talk with Bjørn? She should've called her dad and asked to go with another team.

"Sadie, what's wrong?" Bjørn's heat drew closer to her side. She stepped away and turned to him.

"So, the reporters wanted to know all about the hero willing to go against orders." Sadie crossed her arms as her emotions from the last hour compounded. Bjørn didn't deserve her to be jumping down his throat, but she just couldn't keep all the hurt, anger, and the smidgeon of doubt in. "You giving them an exclusive when we get back?"

"What?" He shook his head, his neck pinking. "What are you talking about?"

"You were awful quick to give the reporters your statement."

"Because they started drilling me about your dad." His hand flew toward the street like the horde was there. "They came at me, popping questions about if your dad should be replaced."

Sadie leaned against the chopper, a sinking feeling leaving her lightheaded. "What did you say?" The whispered question shook out of her.

Rowdy whined and nosed Bjørn's arm. The traitor. The dog was supposed to comfort her. Bjørn rubbed behind Rowdy's ear, none of his frustration translating to his touch.

"That your dad was the perfect man for leading this search." He took a step closer. "That I'm honored to be a part of his team." He closed the distance between them with another step and reached for her aching hand. "And when I saw you flatten that jerk and didn't need me, I knew staying and fighting for your dad's reputation would be more important to you."

The rub of his thumb against her knuckles made her knees tremble. His words both terrified and elated her, making her dizzy. If Jim Miller pushed hard enough, he could ruin her dad. With the reporters' questions and Dad's disapproval of Bjørn, Bjørn could've told them he'd thought it better to keep searching and cut her father's leadership off at the knees.

But once again, Bjørn had pushed aside any bad feelings between him and her dad to make the situation better. He lifted her hand and brushed soft kisses against her bruised knuckles. Her stomach flipped.

"You're wrong, Bjørn Rebel." Her breath that had been bottling up in her chest came easy.

He lifted his eyebrow in question. "Not possible."

She chuckled softly and leaned forward. "I do need you."

His gaze pinned her as they focused with intensity. He cupped her cheeks and captured her lips in a kiss that seared to her very soul. With Bjørn, she felt cherished, but more than that, he respected her. He might not swoop in the instant trouble churned, because he trusted her abilities to handle her own problems. But she could also count on him when she did need him.

A car horn beeped, and Bjørn smiled against her lips. "Looks like we have to go to work."

She kissed him again with a disappointed sigh. "Yeah."

He pulled away and waved at a man getting out of his truck before turning back to her. "What was the boxing match over?"

She swallowed, suddenly embarrassed to hash it out. She peeked a glance at the man digging in the backseat of his truck and determined to rush the words out before he joined them. Puffing out her cheeks, she blew out a frustrated breath.

"That was my ex." She cringed, and Bjørn shifted, crossing his arms. "He dumped me when he found out about my scars." She resisted the urge to rub her arms. "He just wanted to prove he was still a jerk."

"What did he say?" Bjørn's voice lowered.

"Just a bunch of nonsense about me being a sob story and you only being with me to gain publicity for your business." She shrugged, hoping the move didn't show how much the words still hurt.

"Why that—" Bjørn's expression turned hard as granite as he clenched his jaw. "Now I wish I had backed you up. I could hold him while you beat the snot out of him."

Her laugh burst out with a snort, and she quickly covered her mouth. Bjørn's entire countenance softened as he smiled at her. She threw her arms around his neck and put all her happiness in the kiss, not caring that a stranger approached and would probably tell her dad when they got back.

The approaching man cleared his throat, and Sadie pulled back with a soft sigh. She moved to step away, but Bjørn snaked his arm around her waist and held her close to his side. The stranger's eyes narrowed as he stopped before them and looked between her and Bjørn.

"Sadie, this is my brother Gunnar." Bjørn looked down at her. "Gunnar, this is Sadie." The tone of his voice held something she couldn't quite pinpoint but sounded a lot like love.

Her neck heated as she tried to contain her smile. "It's nice to finally meet you."

"So," Gunnar said, a scowl on his face as he dropped his bag to the ground. "You're the reason we can't get any work done."

Chapter Nineteen

Sadie stared out the window through the sheeting rain, scanning the coastline for any sign of the kids or their vessel. Darker clouds built along the southern horizon, lightning flashing in the almost black. Drew, Bo, and Craig had showed up a minute after Gunnar, and they'd been out searching for over two hours. They still had seen no sign of the kids. Neither had any other team, which filled her with so much dread her fingers felt frozen to the window where she gripped it.

"Bjørn, remember that rafting trip growing up where we got lost?" Gunnar's question came over the headset.

He'd scared the snot out of her with his whole cranky brother act. The worry that she and Bjørn had opposition from both families had turned her insides into a knot. When Gunnar had followed the scowling with a wide smile and brotherly hug, her heart almost couldn't take the support.

"Yeah." Bjørn glanced back at his brother, sitting next to her.

"Remember how we took the wrong creek?" Gunnar traced his finger on the map in his lap, and Sadie scooted over so she could see what he was thinking.

"You think they went the wrong way?" Bjørn shook his head. "Miller said his son knows this area inside and out."

"Yep." Gunnar glanced at Sadie, giving her a what do you think look. "We did too. But remember, Julie and that girl you were dating came. The annoying one that giggled at every word you said."

"She did not." Bjørn scoffed, but Gunnar nodded, then made a gagging face.

Sadie's smile hurt her cheeks as she bit her bottom lip to keep from laughing.

"Anyway, distraction and all, we took the wrong creek." Gunnar followed the coastline farther south from Seward and tapped an island outside of the current search area.

Sadie nodded. "That might be possi—"

"Rebel, this is Chief." Dad's voice cut her off through the headset.

"Go ahead, Chief," Bjørn answered.

"Big storm is coming up fast." Frustration coated every single word her dad said. "We have to call everyone in."

She gritted her teeth against his anguish. Miller wouldn't let this ride. He'd have someone's head.

Bjørn turned back to her and Gunnar. "How far out of the way are you thinking?"

Gunnar crouched between the two seats and showed Bjørn the map. Bjørn's cheek muscle popped. He glanced out the window toward the building weather.

He'd already said he wanted to help her dad, but would he challenge orders again?

"Chief, this is Rebel." Bjørn swallowed, his gaze grabbing Sadie's with such determination shining from him. She knew he'd go against orders if he had to.

She took a deep breath and nodded. If Bjørn thought he could fly through the weather, they needed to keep going. Even if doing so brought trouble on her dad.

"Go ahead, Rebel." Her dad's voice fired back, causing her pulse to pound like the fast rotors whirling above them.

Thump-thump-thump.

"We have an idea we'd like to check out." Bjørn kept his eyes on her. "Might be nothing, but we're gonna swing wide around the tip of Montgomery Island and come home along the south coast."

Anyone listening who understood the area would know it wasn't just an alternate way home. It was miles out of the way. The silence hung in the cockpit for an eternity, and her palms slicked with sweat. She begged her dad to trust Bjørn. Begged that they were right, and the kids had gone off course.

"Copy that." No hesitation colored her dad's tone. "Keep us posted. Chief out."

"Will do. Rebel out." Bjørn gave Sadie a triumphant smile and turned forward.

He swung the chopper toward Montgomery Island, and they all settled back into their seats. The farther south they flew, the harder the rain pelted against the windows. A gust of wind rocked them sideways, and Rowdy whined, laying his head in her lap.

Please don't puke all over me.

Her stomach heaved as the chopper dipped again. She might be the one getting sick before her dog did. Lightning flashed less than a quarter mile away. Thunder boomed almost simultaneously. Rowdy whined again, pawing her knee.

"It's okay, buddy." She rubbed behind his ears.

"There!" Drew hollered from the copilot's seat. "Dang it. I lost it."

Sadie strained to see through the downpour. A glimpse of white against the black rock caught her eye. She lifted her binoculars and frantically searched. Was it just a wave stirred up from the storm or the hull of a boat?

Another flash of light brightened the area, followed by a deafening *boom*. The hairs on her arms stood as residual electricity snapped the air.

"That was close." Bo's eyes were wide on his face as he looked across the cabin at her.

Nodding, she swallowed the fear down and brought the glasses back up to her eyes. She methodically searched along the coastline, praying she'd see some sign of the kids. She passed white squeezed between rocks and swung back to it.

"I see it." She explained where it was to the others as she followed the terrain inland. Red flashed, and she sucked in a breath. "I see them. Just above the boat in the trees."

"Got them." Bjørn's voice sounded strained for the first time, and her eyes shot to him.

His muscles were tight as he flipped switches.

"There's only three." Gunnar's words yanked her attention from Bjørn to the kids.

Ice slid under her skin, lodging itself just below the

surface. Three teenagers stood in a small clearing, waving their arms wildly above their heads. She scanned the forest behind them, looking for a sign of someone.

"Base, this is Rebel." Bjørn nosed the chopper toward an outcropping of rocks a half click from the kids.

Gunnar unbuckled and grabbed the medical bag stashed in the storage area. She hated this part of search and rescue, when dread overshadowed the joy of finding the lost. She tightened her hold on Rowdy's collar as the chopper bucked. Gunnar braced himself against the metal roof.

"This is Base, go ahead." Her mom's voice broke through the headset, and, for some reason, the sound made Sadie want to cry.

"We've found the—"

A deafening crack vibrated around them. All her hairs stood on end as the air filled with electricity. Alarms beeped and buzzed. Panic climbed up her throat. The chopper shuddered, the coastline spinning out of view.

"Hang on!" Bjørn yelled over the headset. "We're going down."

The island spun back into view as the chopper lurched. Sadie squeezed her eyes shut and wrapped her arms around Rowdy's neck. Would they crash into the rocks or drown in the frigid ocean? Her body trembled as she tucked the dog closer to her, though any protection she gave didn't mean a thing as they hurled to their deaths.

Chapter Twenty

BJØRN CURSED low and pressed the left rotor pedal to stop the spin. Nothing. Great. The rear rotor blade had malfunctioned. They wouldn't make it.

"Come on, Annie. Work with me," he muttered, lifting the collective in his left hand to gain enough altitude to set her down on the rocks instead of crashing into them as he closed the throttle to stop the rotation.

The collective felt like a two-ton boulder in his hands as it fought against him. He gritted his teeth and pulled up on the control harder as he eased the cyclic in his right hand forward. The skids scraped across the rocks with an eerie sound that raced along his skin and settled in his gut. With a thunk, he set the bird down and sighed. His hands shook as he flipped switches to power down, then turned the alarms off.

The silence that followed bunched his muscles even more, and he turned to scan the others. "Everyone okay?"

His gaze stopped on Sadie as she peeled herself from around Rowdy. Her skin was so pale he could see her veins as she turned her head to look out the window. She took a deep breath, her fingers trembling as she uncurled them from Rowdy's collar.

"We're good." Gunnar rotated his shoulders and neck.

Bjørn turned forward and toggled the radio. "Base, this is Rebel."

Dead air. He switched to another channel.

"Base, this is Rebel."

Nothing. He tried again with the same result. The lightning strike must've knocked the communications out. Like it fried everything else. He growled low and slammed the rest of the controls off.

His jaw hurt from clenching his teeth, and a headache built at the back of his head. He'd have to figure out just how bad the chopper was later. Nothing mattered right now but the kids.

He pulled up his hood and pushed his door open. Rain hit his face with chilling force. Lightning struck a hundred yards away. The boom of thunder shook beneath his feet and hurt his ears. They needed to get away from the chopper. Its metal was like a giant lightning rod.

He secured the strops over the skids as best he could to the rocks, grabbed his gear, and rushed after the others. The teens met them at the tree line, looking soaked and wrung out. The girl, Callie Reed, threw herself into Sadie's arms and bawled.

"You're missing someone." Gunnar's short, efficient words shot through the wind.

Callie cried harder while the two guys froze. The blond one shook his head, his eyes closing in anguish before he dropped his chin to his chest. The other swallowed, looked back toward where they'd come from, then turned back to the rescuers.

"Dex fell." A boom of thunder added grisly emphasis to the second kid's words.

"Where?" Gunnar stepped closer.

"Inland." The blond guy lifted his head, anguish evident in the twisting of his face. "We were hiking back after we couldn't find the lake. Dex slipped on the wet rocks and … and fell to the bottom."

Sadie patted Callie, then pushed her up. "Cody, do you have camp set up?"

"Yeah," the second guy, Jim Miller's son Cody, said, pointing his thumb over his shoulder. "We have some tents."

"Good. Callie needs to get dry and warm." She glanced at Gunnar, then at Bjørn, before turning back to the teens and taking the lead. "Do you remember where he fell?"

Cody rubbed his hand over his mouth. The other kid, Tim Reed, if the fallen kid was Dexter, looked at Cody, his eyes narrowing at Cody's hesitance. Gunnar peeked at Bjørn, and Bjørn gave a quick nod. Yeah, he felt it. Something was off with this group.

"I think I remember." Tim turned from Cody.

"No, I'll take them." Cody stepped forward and touched Callie's shoulder. Callie flinched and took a small step away. "You stay with Cal and make sure she gets warm."

What exactly had happened here? They'd have to figure it out later. Bjørn turned to Drew and the cameramen.

"You guys stay with these two while we go look for the kid." Bjørn pointed to the chopper. "I'll grab the

SAT phone. We'll need you to try to get a hold of base."

"Do you mind if I come and film?" Bo asked, quickly rushing through the rest of his words. "Not for the show or anything. You might be able to use the film for training purposes. I'll help, of course."

Bjørn glanced from Sadie to Gunnar. Both shrugged, so Bjørn gave Bo a quick nod and rushed back to the chopper to get additional gear. He hopped into the cabin and pulled things from the storage.

"I can't believe we found them," Sadie said as she grabbed climbing ropes and hung them over her neck so they rested across her body. "I hope Dexter's not dead. It will devastate his parents."

Her cheeks were still pale, making her freckles pop. Worry pulsed from her in waves. She handed gear to Gunnar who took it and headed back toward the group.

Bjørn jumped from the chopper and gave Sadie's shoulder a quick squeeze. "Whatever has happened, we'll find him and take him home."

Her eyes filled with tears, and her lower jaw shifted to the side. She gave him a nod and swiped her cheek. Heat filled him and pushed away the cold the rain and the situation had settled on him. Man, he loved her. As ridiculous as that seemed, since they'd only known each other a short time, he couldn't deny it. He squeezed her shoulder again and grabbed the rest of the gear.

After settling the cousins in camp with Drew and Craig, Bjørn and the rest of the team followed Cody Miller toward the center of the island. They hiked in silence for about a mile, gaining elevation with each step. The terrain changed from green trees to rocky slopes, and Cody slowed his pace as he scanned the area. His step hesitated, then he hitched his pack higher and pushed on.

The kid had to be exhausted. They'd been stuck out here for three days. From the little information they'd gathered as they'd settled the others in camp, Dexter's accident had happened on the morning of the second day of their trip. For a bunch of nineteen- and twenty-year-old friends, that had to have freaked them out.

Rowdy barked, turning Bjørn to look behind him where Sadie followed. The dog sniffed the area Cody had paused at, his nose wiggling from side to side as he searched. He moved closer to the edge, then pawed at the loose dirt along the cliff before lying down and whining. Bjørn rushed back to Sadie just as she kneeled at the edge and peered down.

"I see him." She shook her head. "I don't see any movement."

Cody stepped up next to Bjørn. "I'm sorry. I guess I didn't remember." His tone was flat and emotionless. Defeated.

"It's okay, man." Bjørn clapped the kid on the shoulder. "Backtracking can be disorienting."

Bjørn peered below and whistled. The craggy cliff side narrowed in long corridors of rock. Dexter sprawled on his back at the bottom, his leg at an odd angle.

Gunnar stepped up next to her and assessed the situation. Bjørn stood back and let his brother do his thing. Finding solutions to the impossible, rescuing people in hairy situations, was how Gunnar had spent the last ten years of his life. He was amazing at it, one of the best.

He set his pack down with the folded backboard strapped to it and pulled things out. Tossing a bag filled with cams pitons at Bjørn, he went back to lining out his gear. Bjørn turned to the rock face on the opposite side of the trail and searched for a good place to anchor to. After hammering three pitons into the cliff side and making sure they were firmly in place, Bjørn clipped on a quickdraw and rope and turned to Gunnar.

"I'll rappel down and assess." Gunnar handed Bjørn a coil of rope. "Toss down two more ropes when I get below. You'll have to lift him out."

Bjørn nodded and got to work setting up for the rappel. When everything was ready, Gunnar clipped in and, without hesitation, disappeared over the edge. The tight squeeze through the rocks had Bjørn worried Gunnar wouldn't fit. Sadie sighed from beside Bjørn as Gunnar touched down.

Gunnar leaned over the kid, then jerked up, his hand cupped over his mouth. "He's alive. I need help."

Bjørn's gaze skipped from Sadie to Bo to Cody and back again. Sadie could climb, but that squeeze through the rocks would kill her. He swallowed and turned to Bo.

"You rappel?" Bjørn fired the question.

"No, man." Bo lifted his hands in apology. "Sorry."

Bjørn closed his eyes as a tenseness hit his gut. Blowing out the breath, he bent close to Sadie, where she still stared at Gunner. He slid his hand along her shoulder and leaned in.

"You're going to have to go down," he whispered in her ear. "I need to stay here to haul Dexter up."

She nodded, though she swallowed big and her fingers gripped the edge of the cliff.

He leaned his forehead above her ear. "You've got this."

Another sharp nod.

Standing to give her space, he dug through the packs for her equipment. Her hands shook as she buckled on the harness. She tried to attach the rope, but her hands trembled too violently. He gently pushed her hand aside and finished getting her hooked up. She glanced over the edge, gave him a weak smile, then stepped backward into the void. Bjørn's heart pounded as he watched her hesitance.

She was too freaked out. He should've figured out another way. Her feet slipped from under her, bashing her into the rock. Bjørn yelled, his heart filling his throat as she lost control and fell.

Chapter Twenty-One

SADIE'S BODY jerked to a stop as the Autoblock knot engaged, swinging her into the cliff with a painful slam. Her protein bar pushed up her throat, but she swallowed it down and gripped the cold rock wall. She squeezed her eyes shut and leaned her head against the surface.

She couldn't do this.

What made her think she could save others when she panicked before she even got to the tight gap?

"You okay?" Bjørn hollered down.

There wasn't worry in his voice like she expected. More … confidence. A sense that she could do this.

She wanted him to be right.

Wanted to push fear aside once and for all.

"Yeah." She looked up. "Just startled me."

He nodded. "The gear is wet from the rain. Just go slow."

Right. The rain. She nodded, though both of them knew the weather had nothing to do with her slip.

She adjusted her grip on the rope and pushed off of the wall, allowing her body to swing out and right itself.

When her feet bounced off the rock, she loosened her hold and continued her descent. The gap drew closer and closer with each bounce, building the fear in her chest until it took up all the space and made it difficult to breathe.

"Doing good." Bjørn's encouragement slid along the rope and warmed her freezing fingers.

She wasn't doing good.

Not even close.

But maybe if she pretended, she could get through without needing rescued herself. She reached the gap and found a handhold. She'd just climb through lickety-split and be on the other side in no time.

Filling her lungs with a shaky breath, she climbed down. The walls pressed in around her, threatening to pin her in. She didn't think about them crushing her. Didn't think about being stuck forever. Just moved one foot lower. Found another hold. Repeat.

Almost there.

The walls tightened their grip, wedging her in. Stopped. Couldn't go down. She reached for a higher hold, but her pack snagged on something. She couldn't move. The fear she'd somehow kept at bay spread through her with a maniacal scream only she could hear, racing her heart to near exploding.

"Sadie, you've got this. Just move up and to your left and your pack will come free." Bjørn was wrong.

She'd never break free.

"Babe, open your eyes and assess the situation." The calm in his voice gave her the courage to listen.

The rough, light brown walls filled her vision, but she forced herself to pivot her head and look.

"There you go." Pride tumbled down on her,

bolstering her. "See the space to your left. If you move that direction, the pack will come free."

He couldn't know that for sure, but she trusted him. Her hand trembled violently as she reached left, her knuckles turning white when her grip took purchase. She pulled herself in that direction.

Nothing.

Numbing terror clawed at her toes, digging its talons into her ankles.

She tried again, pushing with her legs. The sound of ripping fabric filled the air, and she lurched up with the momentum. Shaking out her feet to kick fear off, she scanned the hole for a better angle. One last breath and she twisted her body, squeezing the rest of the way through.

She rappelled fast to the ledge Gunnar waited on. Her knees almost buckled with relief when she landed. Gunnar's face held admiration as he stepped to her, gave her a brotherly side hug, and a knock on the helmet.

"Good job." He took her pack and bent over Dexter. "He's broken his leg and has a blunt trauma to the head. Biggest concern is hypothermia."

"So, we set up a bivouac? Wait for Bjørn to get his chopper?" Sadie wiped the rain from her face.

"No. The bird is toast." Gunnar leaned back, looking up the cliff. "We need to haul him up and get him to camp. Get him dried and warm. No telling how long rescue will be."

She questioned if they should move Dexter, but Gunnar was the expert. She did what she could to help, praying the entire time she wouldn't freak out on the way up like she had going down. After bracing Dexter's leg and neck, they put him in a sleeping bag. Gunnar rigged up a cradle of sorts that would haul Dexter up. While he did that, Bjørn tossed down two more ropes for the climb up.

"I'll go ahead and guide him. You stay here and belay." Gunnar checked her gear. "When we get to the top, you climb up."

"Got it." Sadie nodded.

She watched, barely breathing, as the two got farther away. Gunnar's skill in maneuvering Dexter through the crack was poetic in its fluidity. Every move rolled into the next without hesitation. Before she knew it, the two crested the ridge, and it was her turn to go. With numb fingers, she reached for the first handhold, then the second, pushing herself to not think and just move. She glanced up, then right back down. Big mistake. Her head spun and her grip loosened.

Bjørn gripped his fingers around the cliff's edge as Sadie swayed against the rope. Hollering at her wouldn't help. Maybe he needed to strap in and rappel down.

He glanced back at Gunnar and the others, getting Dexter secured to the backboard. The Miller kid looked freaked, his wide-eyed gaze darting from Dexter to the edge like he couldn't believe his friend had actually survived. His stare landed on the edge where Sadie's rope went over and hardened.

Nope. Bjørn wouldn't do the hero bit unless absolutely necessary. For one, Miller's kid would probably make a big deal about it to anyone who wanted to hear about the rescuer needing saved. And two, Sadie would hate it if he stepped in. She knew how to climb. She just needed to focus through the fear.

He peered down the cliff, his mouth dry, though the rain still pounded around them. She'd steadied herself and had made it to the tight spot. He held his breath, willing her through. It whooshed out with a laugh as she slid up the crack without hesitation.

"Good job, babe," he yelled down at her.

Within no time, she pulled herself over the ledge. Her wide smile had warmth spreading through his muscles and seeping into his bones. The chill from the downpour was forgotten. He pulled her to him and kissed her quickly.

"You're amazing," he whispered in her ear before he pulled back and helped her unhook.

She put her hands on her cheeks, her lips still wide with joy. Her eyes moved to Dexter, and all the joy vanished. He'd find a way to celebrate her win over fear when they got home. Now, they needed all their focus on getting Dexter safe.

They packed up the gear and made it back to camp in half the time it took them to get to Dexter. Bjørn let Drew and Sadie help Gunnar settle Dexter into a tent. Drew hadn't been able to get the SAT phone to work, so it was up to Bjørn to get them out of there. With the winds still blowing, it was unlikely the coast guard or anyone else could fly out.

As he emerged from the trees where his chopper sat, he stopped on the rocks and stared at his Annie. His head shook in disbelief, and his heart thudded dully in his chest. The lightning strike had sheered off the back rotor blade. They wouldn't be flying anywhere.

Couldn't he catch a break? He stomped to the bird.

Psychotic terrorists had blown up his first chopper. Now this one had thousands of dollars worth of damage. That was just what he saw on the outside. There was no telling what kind of damage he'd find once he started digging.

He huffed out his anger. At least they'd survived. A busted bird was better than being dead.

He climbed inside and flipped on the radio. Nothing. Growling, he made his way through the electrical system. His ribs grew tighter around his lungs with each check he did. Not only were they not flying out of there, but he doubted he could get the radios working to call in a rescue. They were stuck with a dying kid and no way to get help.

Chapter Twenty-Two

SADIE PULLED the second sleeping bag up over Dexter's chest as he shivered again. He hadn't woken since they'd found him, and she was beyond worried. The storm rapped against the tent's side, making it shudder violently.

She sighed, rubbing her fingers over her dry eyes. She'd told Gunnar to go sleep an hour ago. He'd worked tirelessly for the last six hours, first hauling Dexter out, then doctoring him up. She'd been embarrassed that she'd fallen asleep when she'd checked on Callie. She'd only meant to rest her eyes but had startled awake two hours later, disoriented and appalled that she'd slept so long.

When she'd rushed into the tent, Gunnar had given her a sad smile that held so much exhaustion in its tight lines, she ordered him to go rest. She had seen no one else, but considering it was two in the morning, she didn't expect to.

She pulled her hands from her face and jumped.

Dexter's bright blue eyes stared up at her. His pupils dilated in fear as his gaze darted around the tent.

"Hey, it's okay Dexter." She laid her hand on his head, hoping the touch would calm him. "I'm Sadie. I'm with search and rescue."

He opened his mouth to speak, but nothing but a croak came out. His lips and chin trembled as he tried again. Sadie's heart broke into a million pieces at what this young man must think and feel.

"Here. You must be thirsty." She moved a medical tube that Gunnar had fashioned into a straw to Dexter's lips. "Go slow, okay?"

He nodded and winced. Taking four gulps, he closed his eyes and sighed. She should go get Gunnar. He'd want to check Dexter over now that he was awake.

She placed her hand over the back of his that he had clenched around the sleeping bag. "I'm going to go get our medic. He'll want to know you're awake."

Dexter grabbed her hand with surprising strength. "The others. Are they safe?"

She smiled, hoping to reassure him, and patted his hand with her other. "They're fine, just resting. It's been a long three days."

"Cody … Cody—" He swallowed, frustration pushing his forehead low over his eyes, and his breathing grew fast and shallow.

"Cody's fine. They all are." Sadie shifted on her knees and placed her palm against his cheek to calm him.

He shook his head and pinned her with a stare. "Cody pushed."

His voice faded, and she leaned over him to hear

him better. There must be some confusion. Her heart-beat pulse roared in her ears, making it hard to hear.

"What?" She hated the shake in her voice.

"Cody pushed me off."

Thunder boomed through the tent, amplifying what Dexter just said to bone-shaking levels.

"Cody pushed you … on purpose?" She couldn't help the question from tumbling out. Why would someone do that?

The zipper to the tent slid open, and she turned to tell Gunnar what Dexter had said. Cody ducked into the tent, letting the door flap in the strong wind. Sadie's stomach bottomed out and her heart raced to near exploding.

"So, you woke up." Cody stared at Dexter as his mouth twisted in an unkind smile.

"Cody, you need to leave, now." The authority in Sadie's voice surprised her.

Cody probably had seventy pounds on her, but she wasn't about to let him hurt Dexter again.

"You couldn't just leave her alone?" Cody asked, ignoring Sadie like she wasn't even there. "You knew I wanted her, but you had to push your way in."

"You're crazy." Dexter's voice came out choppy between his quickening breaths. "She doesn't want you. Never did."

Sadie shifted her legs to a better position. Her shoulders bunched tight and arms tingled. This guy was nuts, pushing someone off a cliff over a girl.

"You're wrong." Cody's angry words rushed through clenched teeth.

Lightning filled the tent with bright light, followed

by a loud *boom*. It flashed against metal as Cody lifted his arm and lunged for Dexter. Sadie screamed, jumping in front of the injured man as the knife came slashing down.

Chapter Twenty-Three

BJØRN ROLLED his shoulders as he walked back to camp. After hours of work, he'd figured out how to reroute the wires to the radio and had called in their location. As soon as the storm lifted enough to fly, the coast guard would come get them. Bjørn breathed easily for the first time since landing.

Voices floated from the tent Dexter fought for his life in, so Bjørn veered course to check in before he changed into dry clothes and crashed for a few. Lightning flashed close, causing Bjørn to duck. His laugh at himself changed to cold terror as Sadie's scream ripped through the air.

Rushing to the tent, he charged in to find Sadie wrestling with Cody Miller. She struggled to hold his hand away as he pushed a knife down toward her. Bjørn dove at Cody, grabbing his arm and wrenching it behind him.

The man bucked and kicked out at Bjørn's legs, but Bjørn held on tight. Cody's yell sent chills down Bjørn's already freezing skin. Sadie scrambled over to Dexter, placing her body between him and the thrashing madman.

Cody wiggled like a worm, pulling and making his way loose from Bjørn's grip. Cody threw his head back, and Bjørn dodged. The jerk's head smashed into Bjørn's cheek, exploding stars across his vision. Sadie took a foot to the chest, flinging her back over Dexter.

Blood pounded in Bjørn's ears as fiery rage rushed through his body. He yanked Cody's hand that still held tight to the knife higher behind him. A loud pop of Cody's shoulder, followed by his blood-curdling scream, filled the air as lightning flashed. Cody didn't give up but kicked out at Dexter even harder.

Sadie pushed off from Dexter, her arm swinging in a powerful arc. Her hook smashed into Cody's jaw just below his ear. He froze, then melted into a heap in Bjørn's arms, knocked out cold.

The flap to the tent ripped to the side, and Gunnar climbed in, his gaze scanning the space. "What happened?"

"Cody tried to kill Dexter." Sadie breathed hard where she slumped next to Dexter. "Pushed Dex off the cliff too."

"Why?" Drew's shocked voice turned Bjørn's attention to the crowd at the tent door.

"I think Cody was jealous of Dexter." Sadie stared down at the guy still hanging on the thin balance between life and death, her words leaving Bjørn stunned. "Jealous that Callie chose Dexter."

"This is all my fault." Callie stepped forward, her voice hitching with tears. "I shouldn't hav—"

"No." Dexter's voice, while weak, held determination. "Not your fault."

"Dex?" Callie held her trembling fingers to her lips.

Dexter motioned for her to come near. Sadie crawled over Cody to get out of the way. Bjørn grabbed her arm and wrapped her in a hug. If he'd been a minute later, she'd probably be dead. He squeezed her tighter to him and buried his face in her hair.

"Callie … I love … you." Dexter's halting words had Callie crying even harder.

She kissed him gently. "I love you too."

Gunnar climbed further into the tent. "Dex, let's check you out."

"Can I stay?" Callie clutched Dexter's hand in hers.

"Absolutely." Gunnar nodded.

"Drew, can you help me get Cody secure in your tent?" Bjørn let go of Sadie, though everything in him wanted to hold her tight.

"Yeah." Drew grabbed Cody's legs and helped Bjørn carry the attempted murderer to Drew's tent.

After making sure Cody couldn't do anymore harm, Bjørn rushed to find Sadie. Lantern light filled the tent she shared with Callie, showing Sadie's silhouette. He unzipped the door and ducked in.

Her hand shook as she cleaned a wound bleeding on her upper arm. His stomach dropped, and he clambered to her side. He took the alcohol wipe from her fingers and gently wrapped his hand around her arm.

"You're hurt." His rough voice gave away the emotion clogging his throat since he heard her scream.

"It's just a scratch." She laughed, but the way her body trembled wasn't funny.

She was right. The wound wouldn't need a bandage, but the thought of what that knife could've done had him huffing out a shaky breath. He finished cleaning it and kissed right above it. Then trailed kisses up to her shoulder and along her neck. She fisted her hand in his shirt, but her kiss on his lips was gentle.

"You okay?" he whispered against her mouth.

"Yeah." She sighed, burying her face in his neck. "I'm just … I'm just so tired and sad. Why would anyone do that?"

"I don't know." He rubbed her back. "Come on, lie down so you can get some rest."

Her grip tightened on his shirt, and her trembling doubled. "I can't."

He held her closer and lay on her sleeping bag. She pulled away just enough to look in his eyes. Hers were bright with tears, and her dark circles showed her exhaustion. He'd never seen anyone more beautiful.

"I love you, Sadie," he whispered, not able to keep the words in.

A tear slipped past her lashes and trailed down her cheek. "I love you too."

Heart soaring higher than he'd ever flown, he gave her a soft, lingering kiss. He might have a chopper busted beyond repair. They might be stranded on a rain-soaked island with a cold-hearted killer. But he'd never been happier than he was with Sadie Wilde in his arms.

Chapter Twenty-Four

THREE DAYS LATER, Sadie stared at the army helicopter as it flew Bjørn's Annie into the Seward airport. Her heart broke for him as it thunked against the ground. When he'd told her he wasn't even sure it was fixable, she'd wanted to cry for his loss. He had insurance, but whether it could be fixed or not, it still ended his first summer tourist season before it got fully off the ground.

She stayed back and watched as he worked with the soldiers sent from Fort Richardson to help transport the broken chopper. She loved the way he moved with efficiency, double-checking everything before he gave the go to release the bird. Him and his checklists.

She chuckled as she remembered him whispering that she blew all his checklists and procedures out of the air. She liked that thought. That she could shake the unshakeable Bjørn Rebel.

He waved as the helicopter took off, headed back to Anchorage. His smile as he walked to her held a sadness she wanted to kiss away. She slid her hands under his jacket and along his sides. His muscles flexed beneath his T-shirt at her touch.

He gently cupped her face and captured her lips in a kiss that held all his disappointment. She ran her hands up his back, pulling him closer. She wanted to ease his frustration but didn't know how to. He growled and changed the angle of his kiss as he pushed his fingers through her hair.

His love flowed over her, threatening to drown her in hope. Muscles stopped working and bones turned to mush. She leaned in for him to hold her up.

The sound of a vehicle approaching pulled them apart. He smiled down at her, gave her another quick kiss, then glanced up at who had arrived. His eyes widened and he cringed.

"Busted." He slid his hand down her arms to thread his fingers with hers.

She turned to see what he meant. Her dad climbed out of his truck, a scowl on his face. She groaned. Could he pick a worse time to show up?

"Sadie. Rebel." Dad stepped up to them, surprising her by extending his hand to Bjørn.

Bjørn jerked but clasped Dad's hand without hesitation. "Sir."

Dad gestured toward the chopper. "You got her back."

"Yeah." Bjørn shook his head. "Not even sure if it'll be worth fixing her. The insurance guys are coming tomorrow."

"Well, I can't wait for you to get back in the air." Dad shoved his hands in his front pockets. "You've been a godsend to our team."

Bjørn's throat bobbed as he shook his head. "I'm just glad I can help."

Sadie's heart swelled with relief and love. Her dad extending the olive branch was a step forward. She slipped her arm around Bjørn's back and leaned into his side.

"Dexter is healing well. They think he'll be able to leave the hospital by the end of the week. Jim's trying everything he can to get Cody out on bail, but doesn't look like it'll happen." What was up with Dad? He wasn't one for chitchat.

"That's good." Sadie crinkled her forehead at her dad's odd behavior.

He sighed, then looked Bjørn straight in the eyes. "Listen, Bjørn, I'm sorry for acting like a jerk and jumping to conclusions about you. It wasn't right, and I'm sorry. I am an overprotective bear when it comes to my daughters."

Bjørn's ribs expanded beneath Sadie's hand as he took a deep breath. "Apology accepted. I'd be the same if I was a dad."

The thought of Bjørn being a father, of holding their baby girl in his strong hands, was an image Sadie wanted to see. One she never thought would come true but seemed possible now. She peeked up at Bjørn as her dad continued.

"Listen, we're having a family barbecue this after-noon. We'd like you to come with Sadie."

Bjørn froze, like the invitation was a car and he was a caribou caught in the headlights. "Thank you, sir."

"Bring that brother of yours too." Dad reached his hand out to shake again, and Sadie parted from Bjørn. "But Rebel ..."

"Yeah?"

"No making out with my daughter while I'm around." Dad speared Bjørn with a look that had red climbing up his neck.

"I'll try, sir." Bjørn gave a strangled laugh and rubbed the back of his neck.

"Really?" Sadie rolled her eyes, stepped up to her dad, and gave him a hug. "Thanks, Dad."

"No, Sadie, thank you for showing me I was wrong." He gave her a squeeze and stepped back. "I'm proud of you." He nodded, his eyes bright and glossy. "Really, really proud."

Shoot. She sniffed and threw herself back in his arms. "I love you."

"Love you, too, squirt." He patted her back, then stepped back, swiping the back of his hand across his cheek. "I told your mom I'd be right back to help. Shindig starts at two."

Bjørn slung his arm over her shoulder as her dad walked back to his truck and drove away. "Well, that was unexpected."

"Yeah." She sighed. "It was."

She leaned into Bjørn, placing her hand over his heart. It pounded steadily against her palm, calling her to him. This unwavering Rebel beside her was a beacon guiding her home. She closed her eyes and let the peace and happiness flood her.

Epilogue

GUNNAR SAT, his back against a picnic table, picking the label off of his soda as he watched Bjørn play croquet with Sadie and her cousin Denali's son, Sawyer. Sadie whacked the ball and sent it bouncing across the yard. When it sailed through the little hoop in the ground, Sadie and Sawyer went crazy, jumping up and down and hugging like they'd just won the Super Bowl. Rowdy and Denali's dog, Hank, ran around the yard in a chase, adding to the chaos.

"It was one hoop." Bjørn threw out his arms, his head shaking in disbelief, causing Gunnar to chuckle. "You still have ten more."

Sadie gave Sawyer one last hug, then sauntered up to Bjørn as the kid took his turn. Bjørn's face shone with a happiness Gunnar hadn't seen since Bjørn first got accepted into SOAR. His gaze never left Sadie, as she said something too low for Gunnar to hear. Bjørn threw his head back in a loud laugh.

The sound settled in Gunnar's gut like he'd drunk too many colas. Once laughter and heated stares had filled his days and his dreams with happiness. Now, the memories taunted him with what he could have had. In the fifteen years since he joined the Air Force, determined to become the best pararescueman the military had seen, the memories of Julie hadn't eased in their barrage of his thoughts.

He grunted at his self in disgust.

If he would've just thrown out the unopened letters from her he'd kept in his pack or deleted the email he'd saved but never read, maybe then she wouldn't haunt him. He wouldn't constantly wonder what would have happened if he hadn't pushed her away to follow his dreams.

Maybe Bjørn was right. Not that Gunnar would tell his brother that. Maybe Gunnar should give Julie a call. Her father had died racing the Yukon Quest earlier that year, and some speculated whether or not she would continue racing in his stead. The articles always referenced her as Julie Sparks, her last name growing up, a fact that had all kinds of hope welling up in his heart.

"Your brother's good for her." Denali plopped down next to him. She smiled as Bjørn made a big fuss about Sawyer getting the ball through the hoop, throwing the kid into a round of giggles.

"She's good for him too." Gunnar twisted the bottle in his hands. "Sawyer's a neat kid. Tall for an eleven-year-old."

"Yeah. He gets that from his father."

"Hmm. Can't wait to see how tall he is." Gunnar figured the man had to be at least six-five with how tall Sawyer already was.

"Yeah, well, you might be waiting a while." Denali's response startled Gunnar. "Sawyer's dad plays hockey in the National Hockey League. He just got traded and probably won't be able to visit for a while."

"I'm sorry."

"It's okay. He's going to come home when he can." Denali's eyes widened as Drew walked through the gate. "Would you excuse me?"

She didn't wait for an answer. Just beelined it for the house. Drew's gaze followed her the entire way, a small smile inching his mouth up on one side.

Gunnar shook his head and turned his attention back to the game. He didn't understand how a man could do what Sawyer's dad had done, leave his responsibilities behind. He watched as Sawyer lined up the mallet for a hit. Gunnar would give anything to have a family around to fill the empty nights. Pain stabbed at the back of his throat.

Hypocrite.

Sure, he hadn't left Julie pregnant, but he'd abandoned her just the same. Their love hadn't just been a silly high school relationship. They had built it on years of friendship and trust that had grown into something he had never moved on from.

They'd both known he would go to the military. It was all he'd ever talked about. Well, that and dog sledding. But in his stupid, youthful selfishness, he'd only seen one way to get to his goal.

It wasn't until he'd gotten into the trenches that he'd realized having a spouse at home supporting your efforts didn't make you weak or divide your attention. The married soldiers had a reason to go home, a way to find rest and hope after hard missions.

Julie wouldn't have been a distraction. Not having her by his side had obstructed his thoughts during down time, always wondering what she was doing. Always remembering the way she'd smiled up at him with such trust.

Gunnar shook his head and pushed off from the table to join Bjørn and Sadie. He couldn't contact Julie. Hope for a second chance blew apart when he'd turned from her tear-stained face and walked away.

Want to continue the Rebel family adventure? Is it too late for a second chance at love for Gunnar? Find out in A Rebel's Promise.

Still not ready to let Sadie and Bjørn go? If you want to get a special bonus scene just for newsletter subscribers, head here: https://BookHip.com/TXFJVVV

Will Sadie's sister and cousins get their happily-ever-afters? Check out Denali's story in Wild About Denali, a sweet romantic comedy.

Also by Sara Blackard

Other Books

Meeting Up with the Consultant

About the Author

Sara Blackard has been a writer since she was able to hold a pencil. When she's not crafting wild adventures and sweet romances, she's homeschooling her five children, keeping their off-grid house running, or enjoying the Alaskan lifestyle she and her husband love. Find out more at www.sarablackard.com

CPSIA information can be obtained
at www.ICGtesting.com
Printed in the USA
LVHW091305080921
697338LV00003B/65

9 781954 301269